ANIMAGE ACADEMY

THE SHIFTER SCHOOL DOWN UNDER

QATARINA & ORA WANDERS

WANDERING WORDS
M E D I A

Dedicated to all our Australian, African, Indian, Korean, Japanese, and European friends who helped us bring these characters to life.

AUTHORS' NOTE

As wanderers, we have traveled to a lot of places and met a *lot* of people. The people and locations in this story are indeed based on those we have met in our travels. All the characters come from different cultures, and we have drawn upon details based on extensive research as well as information learned and shared from their real-life counterparts. All this with permission, of course.

Please know we have respect for all cultures, and if any character details come across as disrespectful, it is absolutely not intended.

This story—even though it takes place in a fantasy setting—addresses many real-life issues like bullying, gaslighting, and bigotry. This is especially present in a teenager's world. The goal here is to speak to these very real issues, but with a different fictional twist. Instead of the students being teased and hated on for their race, gender identity/sexual orientation, or upbringing, they are segregated by shifter species and status on the food chain.

The cultural differences play a big part here as the students—predator and prey alike—experience all kinds of conflict before they can achieve unity.

The elite rule classroom, but find out what really makes them elite...

— QAT & ORA

Where the heck was her other shoe? They were both right beside her bed last night before she turned in, and now she was staring at one naked foot.

"Mom, it's not in the closet!"

Ava could swear she heard her mother cuss. She wasn't sure, but that sounded suspiciously like "Dammit!" Then her mother yelled back, "I meant the hallway closet!"

"Oh," Ava muttered and shuffled out of her room. Buster spotted her immediately and began to bark. Well, she couldn't really call that barking —short little squeaks rather. He lunged his entire twelve pounds on her, nearly knocking Ava down on her butt because she couldn't balance her weight evenly wearing only one shoe. Stupid little pug.

"Hey, Boy..." she cooed, ruffling his tawny, fluffy ears.

His little pink tongue snaked out, covering her face in saliva.

"Ew, Buster, you're so gross! Wait, did you steal my shoe again?"

The dog appeared decidedly innocent, his chocolate brown eyes daring her to doubt his honesty. She plopped him down on the floor and moved on to the hallway closet. She could hear her mother clattering in the kitchen.

Ava didn't have the extra energy to search for anything that wasn't already in the bag. Lying awake all night would do that to a person. For weeks, she'd prepared, alternating between excitement and utter debilitating terror. Then, two weeks ago, it arrived in the mail.

Her mother, Lucy, who was just as excited, couldn't wait as she tore the puffed-up envelope open. Leave it to the oldest shifter academy to use an old-style scroll, crossed with a red ribbon and sealed with a crested griffin head.

"What does it say?" her mother had asked, peeking over her shoulder at the letter.

Ava had taken her precious time unwrapping

the scroll, biting off the seal with her teeth, drawing the ribbon loose...

"Well?" her mother had prompted when she couldn't take Ava's silence anymore.

"I got in," Ava had whispered, disbelief pumping through her.

"What? You did?" Then pride replaced the astonishment in Lucy's voice. "Oh, my baby, of course you did!"

Then Ava was swept into a hug that still hurt her ribs.

She rifled through the closet, shifting piles of coats and hats. Yep, there it was, the other half of the only sensible pair of shoes she had: black high-top Converse. The rest were tottering heels her mother insisted were appropriate for a "classy woman." She snickered—there was nothing remotely classy about her this morning, not unless she counted her bird-nest hair and the dried drool across her face.

"Found it!" she yelled back. With Buster yipping at her feet, Ava made her way toward her bedroom. She checked the hallway mirror: no, that was no classy woman staring back at her. She rubbed at the dark circles beneath her eyes as though that would get them off, but she was pretty sure she merely made them darker.

As she trudged the rest of the way to her room,

she resisted the urge to sink down on the hard-wood floors, cuddle Buster, and just cry.

She knew she should be happy about today, and earlier she was. Ava had run around their small apartment, gathering the stuff she needed and even a bunch of other things that were absolutely useless. She'd thrown them with gusto into the open suitcase on her bed.

"You've got to hurry! The portal only stays open for a short time, Sweetie." Her mom peeped into her doorway. "Uh, did an earthquake hit your room?!" she shrieked, opening the door fully.

"Mom! You're supposed to knock!" Ava contested, miffed but unfazed by her unacceptable mess.

"Ava? What have you been doing? Not packing, evidently."

Instead of answering, Ava let the waterfall of tears she'd been trying so hard to hold back pour out.

Her mother froze in the doorway, obviously not expecting this. "Oh, Sweetie..."

"Mom, I can't seem to get anything right." Ava sniffled between breaths. "I don't even know what I'm supposed to take or leave behind. I mean, what should I take to the best school on the planet? What if they hate me on sight? What if I don't make any friends? What if I flunk all my classes?

Why did they even accept my application, Mom, why? I could hardly be considered a real shifter! I'm definitely not like the others."

Lucy stared at her daughter, speechless. This had to be the first time Ava had doubted herself since she was born. Was this coming from her daughter, who didn't shed a single tear on the first day of kindergarten? This was unfamiliar territory for her as a mother—how was she supposed to console a sniveling teenager?

Carefully, Lucy stepped through the piles of clothes on the floor, and she plonked down on her daughter's bed, opened her arms, and Ava fell into them, shoulders quivering.

"Mom, what if I mess this up? I don't even think I'm really supposed to be there. What if it's all a mistake?"

"Hey, listen to me, Ava, you are the best, most talented shifter I know."

Ava wiped her nose and peered up at her mother through long lashes. "You're only saying that 'cause you're my mother...."

"What? No! Tell me, who has had straight A's throughout high school?"

"I did," Ava muttered.

"Okay, who won all the track championships?"

A little smile peeked through. "I did."

"That's right, and who's phone won't stop

ringing and beeping?" Lucy rolled her eyes as she said it.

"Mine..."

"Exactly. I've never seen anyone who worked harder at being the best at everything. People are drawn to you like a magnet, and I can bet anything it will be the same at your new school. You'll show them just how likable you are."

"But, Mom, this is different."

"It is *not*, they are shifters, too, with the same abilities—" Her breath caught in her throat.

"Super cool abilities. Way cooler than mine." Ava mumbled the last few words.

Lucy's brows creased worriedly. Ava knew that expression all too well.

Uh oh. This was worse than Ava had thought, and she'd be lying if she said she wasn't even more concerned now. Ava had always been reasonably confident and comfortable in her own skin, sure. More so than other girls she knew, but now, even her own mother looked worried about her and her abilities (or lack thereof).

Before Ava's thoughts could spiral further, Lucy interrupted them. "You are special, too, Sweetie. If you don't know that, eventually, you will realize it. The school wouldn't have accepted you other-wise." Lucy pecked Ava lightly on her forehead and stood from the bed. "Okay, now that that's all cleared up"—she ignored the death stare Ava tossed at her—"I can help you get ready. Seriously, we don't have much time before the portal closes, and it won't open for another month. So chop chop."

Ava raised an eyebrow. "Chop...chop?"

"It means hurry up—common phrase."

"Yeah, about a million years ago."

Lucy shook her head, picking up an open box.

Less than an hour later, the room was tidy, her suitcase packed, her cream carpet visible again, her bed made, and her closet emptied.

"You still have time for a quick shower, and I'll get your breakfast ready," Lucy offered.

"And I'll get ready for social suicide," Ava grumbled as she slinked over to the bathroom and slammed the door. Her mother could say whatever she wanted, but, at the end of the day, she—Ava—would be the one thrown to the wolves—literally.

2

"You're special." Ava mimicked her mom's voice as she stepped out of her shower, picked up a dry towel, and wiped the steam off her mirror. Staring at her reflection, Ava groaned. She knew she wasn't bad looking, but she was no beauty queen. She was skinny, pale, and awkward with her lanky limbs. Not many curves either. Not requiring much work, her cascading brown hair did its own thing, and curled under naturally at the tips. She wasn't a fan of the drab dirt-brown color, though. Her eyes were deep turquoise—very feline. She caressed her cheekbones—they completed her heart-shaped face, down to her pouty, full lips.

Sure, she could be much worse off, and she'd be blind not to notice all the times boys fell over themselves trying to get her attention. But she had no idea what they saw in her.

"Ava? Are you dying in there?"

Her mom was also a drama queen. That's where Ava got it from.

"Be right there." She yanked her button-down Oxford shirt off the hanger on the back of her door and stuffed her arms into it as fast as she could, trying to cuff the sleeves up to her elbows as she simultaneously pulled on her jeans. It didn't work. She tumbled over instead.

"Gah!" she grunted out as she reassembled herself into a standing position, finished securing her jeans, and returned to cuffing her shirt sleeves as she made her way to her sneakers. It was too hot to be wearing a long-sleeve shirt, but Ava was used to it by now. She always kept her arms covered to hide her shifter mark.

Every shifter develops a shifter mark on his or her upper right arm during adolescence: a solid black silhouette shape of whatever animal they shift into. All young shifters wait anxiously to find out what theirs will be. And Ava's came as no surprise—a tabby cat, just like her mother. Lucy wore hers proudly, unashamed of what she was. But for Ava it was a different story. Especially because she was still only sixteen. Adult shifters could pass off their marks as tattoos. She couldn't, so she had been hiding hers since it showed up three years earlier.

She met her mother in the kitchen and scarfed down her breakfast of bacon and eggs at an impressive speed. She knew she needed all the energy she could get for the trip.

Lucy called her an Uber, and when the driver arrived, he appeared appropriately confused when she told him the destination, especially considering the number of bags and all.

"Are you sure you don't mean the airport or train station?" he questioned.

"No, take her to Sunny Isles," Lucy insisted.

"Sunny Isles *beach*?" the man repeated, obviously still unsure.

Ava noticed the betraying vein ticking on her mother's forehead and cut in before Lucy could open her mouth again. "Yes, please, help me with the bags."

The confused driver shook his head as they loaded the bags into the trunk. Once the trunk was jam-packed, Ava turned to Lucy and threw her arms around her. "I'm gonna miss you so much, Mom."

Lucy squeezed her back...for a little too long (the driver reminded them by clearing his throat). "Remember the instructions? You should be able to find your contact person easily, but if you get lost, call me, okay?"

"Okay, Mom." Ava choked, trying not to cry again. She wouldn't see her mom again for almost a year. The academy didn't even take holiday breaks. She dropped her hands and stepped into the waiting car, then turned to watch her mother wiping tears from her eyes. She watched until Lucy faded to a tiny heaving black dot.

Ava rested her head against the window, letting the cool glass pane reduce the pounding in her head—crying always made her head hurt. This was about to be a complete makeover from her life in Miami. She was soon to be at the bottom of the food chain.

"What's a pretty girl like you doing at the beach this early in the morning?" The driver tried to make conversation. Nice enough guy—overweight with graying hair.

Ava just rolled her eyes.

"Not very talkative, are you?" he kept trying.

Ava pressed her head against the pane again. A chatty Uber driver wasn't what she needed right now. No, she wanted to go back home, to be with her mother, to plan for college, to... Okay, who was she kidding? This was her dream, her ambition, all she could think about for years! She'd written hundreds of practice applications, imagined acceptance letters, but she never really believed she would get in. She should be celebrating. What the heck was wrong with her?

She rubbed the ache in her forehead—the pounding had increased. She bit down on her lower lip, hard, wiggled in her seat, removed her head from the pane, let her shoulders slump back. Her breathing was getting heavier. The heat was spreading down her neck to her chest. She put the back of her hand to her forehead—oh god, it could fry an egg.

No, this couldn't be happening right now. She was having a panic attack. And if she lost control, she was likely to shift. *No, no, no....*

She wrapped her arms around herself, hugged her knees in close, blood pounding painfully in her head. Her extremities started to tingle.... *NO!*

The car slowed to a crawl. Why was he stopping?

She opened her throbbing eyes to slits. She had to blink in quick succession to clear her vision and force her eyeballs to stay down. The vehicle was nose-to-bumper with another car—a Mercedes—they had hit the early morning traffic jam. *Ugh.* Her feet dragged upward, curled on the threadbare seat. A tail had started to sprout—she could feel it poking the inside of her jeans—and she could see fur sprouting on the backs of her hands.

Focus, Ava, focus!

A groan shot its way to her lips, but she tamped it down along with her quivering legs.

The driver mistook her reaction for annoyance. "Don't worry. It won't take long; we'll be on our way soon."

"Hmmm," was all Ava could mutter, squeezing her compact frame into a ball.

"Supposed to cut back now," he prattled on, apparently not hearing her distress behind him. "They widened the road awhile back...." He peeked at her via the rearview mirror, and his eyes widened at her blanched face. "You okay there, Miss?"

"I'm—I'm fi—ine." *Just growing fur and a tail. Nothing to see here.*

"Miss?"

"I said I'm fine!" Ava snapped, then caught herself. "Sorry, I'm okay." She forced herself to take a deep breath. Color flooded her entire face as she tried to gain control.

Just breathe...you got this.

She felt her pulse slow back down, and the tingling dissipated. She looked back down at her hands. No more fur. The car zoomed off into another lane, going faster. Her phone bumped off her lap onto the floor, dragging her attention back to the present.

Thankfully, the driver hushed, and she was glad for the silence.

Outside, girls in bikinis strutted along, a few guys dragged surfboards, and shiny coffee houses came into view. She was almost there. Leaning back, she imagined what her new school would be like. Sure, she'd seen brochures, and this year's directions (the portal was different every semester), but she'd never been there.

"We're here," the driver announced, staring back at her in the rearview mirror.

Ava jerked out of her thoughts. "Oh, right, thank you."

She stepped out of the car, still a little shaky. The comforting sound of the crashing waves hit her before anything else. She took a deep inhalation of the ocean smell as she moved to the trunk to help unload. While setting one of her bags down on the sidewalk, she noticed a man inching closer and closer to them. He held a small clipboard that he scrutinized, then stared at her.

Had to be her point-of-contact person. She offered a tiny wave in his direction.

He squinted back.

"That's the last of them." The driver looked at her expectantly. He was referring to her bags.

Oh, right, she should tip him. She reached into her purse for a twenty and handed it to him—a pretty fat tip, for sure. He was soon out of sight in a cloud of sand.

A smile broke through her lips as she watched him go, despite the panic rising in her chest. Then she turned toward the man with the clipboard and approached him.

"Hi, I'm Ava Carrington." She didn't offer her hand because they were full of bags.

"Paul," the man introduced himself as he took her heaviest bag from her. "You ready?" He smiled kindly, tucked the clipboard under the arm holding her suitcase, and extended his right hand.

With one of her hands now free, she took his outstretched hand in hers, firmly. "I am."

He grabbed another smaller satchel off her shoulder. "Then follow me."

He took long strides, and even though she wasn't particularly short, she still struggled to keep up with him.

"You're the last one in. We almost left thinking you chickened out on us." It didn't seem like he was joking. His accent was distinctly Australian— she wouldn't have understood a word he'd said if he'd spoken faster.

Leave her? Seriously? "Traffic. Sorry." She tried

not to pout but felt that telltale bottom lip protrude.

"Yeah, Miami can be crazy," he agreed.

He appeared too young to be a teacher; too old to be a student. Ava wondered if he was just the chaperone and nothing else. In the waves, his dark hair, slicked back from his forehead, blew around haphazardly in the chilly winds. He had to be at least six feet tall, and with that accent, didn't seem like he spent time in the U.S. at all.

"Do you stay at the school?" she blurted.

He acted as if he hadn't heard her.

Alrighty then.

Together they walked along the deserted shore. A sporadic runner passing in the distance. A lazy red ball in the sky peeking out of the clouds. The promise of a beautiful day—too bad she was going to miss it.

A little ahead, she could make out a lineup of whitewashed boats tottering on the water. Their destination? How many others were coming on the trip with her?

When they got to the boat, she climbed up first, dragging her bag behind her. Then she stood to wait for Paul.

"You packed as if you're staying away for years. Isn't this a bit much?" he teased.

"What?" She tilted her head to the side. "I like to be prepared. Sue me."

"Yeah, seems like it." He heaved the last bag up to the deck and climbed in after her.

Ava looked around, confused. "Um, where are the others?"

He just snorted. Why wouldn't he answer her questions? When he started the engine, it coughed and came to life. Ava sat back on the bench, ready for an unknown adventure.

3

They rode the winds for at least thirty minutes before Paul switched off the engine. Ava looked around, searching for the next step. How the heck were they supposed to get through this portal?

The boat rocked softly in the electric-blue waters. To make it even more awkward, Paul was sitting there, well, actually reclining, on the bench opposite her, calmly picking his nose.

So gross.

"Um, what are we waiting for?" she asked, unable to sit still a second longer. She pushed her hair out of her eyes to give her hands something to do. She was that anxious.

The wind whistled even louder in her ears. Paul smiled again, and scrunched his left sleeve up, revealing a Rolex. "Should be here in five... Four... Three... Two..."

Ava's head swung to the right—a humming sound was coming from that direction.

The waters roiled and danced around menacingly. Whatever made the noise was coming straight for them. Terror surged through her, and she gripped her seat with both hands. "Paul," she screamed. "We gotta move!"

"Yes, we most certainly do. No kidding." He jumped to his feet.

"Whoa..." Ava's eyes got even bigger. "Oh my God!" The boat tottered dangerously from side to side. The only thing Ava could imagine doing was holding on for dear life. Was this supposed to be happening? The brochure had mentioned nothing about this horror!

Paul still seemed as calm as could be. "Grab your bag," he said to her over his shoulder as he grasped the two bigger bags, leaving her with only the smaller one to haul on her own.

The boat rocked faster. Ava sat right where she was because standing would mean falling in the water. She didn't trust her balance at all.

Just as fast as it had crept up on them, the humming suddenly ceased. "Okay, let's go now." Paul stepped over the bench and walked around her.

Not willing to stand up, Ava looked ahead, squinting her eyes for the source of the humming, then looked behind her. She didn't have to look far because the monstrosity was now right in front of her, less than ten feet from the boat she was currently sitting in.

She saw a transparent hole in the water, or maybe translucent was a better word—a rounded, deep black abyss. Kind of how she always pictured the Bermuda Triangle. "We're not supposed to step into that, are we?"

"That we are, Mate. That we are." Amusement was apparent in his voice. "Throw your bags in first. You don't want them to land on top of you, now do you?"

She glared at him suspiciously as she whipped her hair back and then tossed her suitcase into the gaping hole. Wanting to appear as comfortable with everything as possible wasn't working for her. She was far from comfortable, and she knew it showed.

The abyss immediately swallowed her bags up. Paul promptly threw the remaining bags after them, then said, "Go, go, go! Don't take all day to think about it."

Doing as he said, she didn't take any time to process. She just threw herself over the edge, leaping into the air, and clumsily tumbling into the hole. She fought the urge to scream like a scared child the whole way down.

As she fell, all she could think about was how much her landing was going to hurt. How she hoped it would be a soft surface. But, to her surprise, she landed perfectly, feet first, on a concrete floor. She flailed her arms helplessly as she did so, but she still didn't fall over. She kept reaching for anything to hold her upright, but there was nothing nearby. Eventually, she realized she could stop struggling because she was perfectly fine.

"It's about time," a female voice grumbled from nearby.

"Certainly took her sweet time getting here," mumbled another voice, this one male.

Finally, looking at her surroundings, Ava realized she was in some sort of hallway. The hallway seemed endless to her, with white light streaming from top to bottom. There were tiny dots all over the hall at one end. As she squinted, Ava realized those tiny dots were actually other students. There were three other students standing close to her. She assumed they were other Americans who had come through the portal with her. Somehow.

Immediately to her right was a girl with gorgeous hair, a shocking pink color and cut short to her jawline. The girl wore a short, animal-printed skirt and a billowing plaid shirt completed with black combat boots. Next to her was a guy wearing a parka and jeans. The parka seemed out of place. Ava couldn't guess what he was wearing under his parka, but she could see wheat-colored hair peeking out around his face from under the hood.

The other boy had dark skin, huge-framed glasses sitting on his rounded nose, and his lower lip was outrageously red. But his upper lip was totally black. What an interesting makeup job. *Okay then.*

She was about to approach the girl with the pink hair when Paul dropped beside her, and she snapped her mouth shut.

"Okay, everyone ready to go?" Paul looked around at the four students.

"Finally," the pink-haired girl griped.

"Stop complaining, Michaela." Paul rolled his eyes. "Not all of you live right next to the beach, remember?" He turned his attention back to Ava. "Oh, Ava, this is David," he said, pointing to the blond guy and then turned and slapped the other guy on the back. "And this is Zeke. You're all from the Miami branch, obviously."

Obviously? Was that really supposed to be obvious? Because it totally wasn't—at least not to her.

Without waiting for a response, Paul continued down the hall, clearly expecting them to follow. When they didn't, he called over his shoulder, "Come on, the others are waiting!"

Ava looked over at the guy called Zeke. He shrugged, picked up his bag, and went after Paul. The others followed suit, so Ava figured she should, too.

"Where are we going?" Ava asked the pink-haired girl—Michaela.

"This must be your first year." Michaela turned her pert nose up. "Explains all the bags."

Okay, so even though her clothes and hair made this girl look fun and cool, she obviously wasn't exceptionally nice. Noted.

Ava kept quiet. She was going to get answers soon, anyway. All she knew was they were underwater now, and that was definitely why the long hallway had no windows—just all the crazy wobbling lights.

As they approached the end, Ava heard voices rising in the distance. They kept getting louder as they got closer. They were coming from all sides. Now Ava could see a sea of students. And she realized Michaela's hair was actually pretty normal around here. Many of the students sported green, yellow, bright red, purple, and even rainbow hair.

Ava suddenly felt out of place with her stupid normal brown hair.

It turned out the humming she'd heard came from a submerged ship. How was that possible? They weren't excessively far below sea level, and she had only been staring out at the ocean for maybe ten minutes when Paul's voice had announced the ship was ready to go.

Ava looked at the submerged ship again and couldn't help her lips parting. She didn't quite allow her jaw to drop exactly, but her mouth was definitely hanging open somewhat. The ship was not a submarine, just a literally *submerged* ship. It looked exactly like a typical cruise ship she would take above the water, but it was somehow down here...*under* the water. She closed her eyes and shook her head. There was no time to try to figure out all the magic being used here.

Following Paul, and the other new students, to the registration desk, Ava edged through the throngs of yelling teenagers, all impatient to get on with their lives.

If only she had such zeal jumping through the portal; maybe she wouldn't have tumbled through it like a baby bird who wasn't ready to leave the nest. Ava cringed at the memory of her own actions.

"Your application ticket, please." A snout-nosed man was staring at her intently from the other side of the registration desk. When she looked up at him, she accidentally let out a bark of astonishment. He had hairy dog ears protruding from the sides of his head. His face was red, probably from repeating the same instructions to all the clueless students.

"Oh, yes." Ava tried to get her bearings again. "Here you go." She handed him her scroll; it was still wrapped in the ribbon and everything. She tried not to stare too fixedly at the hair sticking from his ears and snout. It was more than a little weird to her.

"Shifting gone wrong." A male voice from behind her startled her out of her thoughts. Her head jerked back. It was a boy, probably about her age, and perhaps the prettiest boy she'd seen in all her life. But that was beside the point.

Pretty, yes, the only word she could think of to describe him. But still not in an unmasculine way. He sported muscular, hulking shoulders, and he was tall. At least six feet. She had to lean her head back to look at him, and she wasn't short.

He was Indian—or at least that would've been her best guess—and gorgeous. But instead of rich black hair one would expect on a handsome Indian boy, his hair was the color of snow. And his catlike eyes could penetrate her soul. They were

26

dark green with gold flecks within them. His sun-kissed skin was a beautiful brown color, and he spoke with a thick accent Ava couldn't quite place.

Ava's eyes zipped up and down his body as he looked back at her. Wait, he had said something, right? What did he say to her again...?

"I said, you can board," the dog-eared man interrupted, pulling her from her semi-trance. She snatched the tickets and her acceptance letter back from his hairy fingers and rushed to the boarding plank, her face burning. That beautiful boy was the kind of guy she usually avoided. Way too attractive to be talking to her, especially now that she was at the bottom of the food chain at this new school. Hopefully, she wouldn't have to talk to him again...ever.

Paul had taken care of her luggage, promising to have it waiting at the school. It made her stomach drop a little to release her bags, wondering if they would make it to her destination. But seeing as how all the other students had done the same, she had let it go.

Besides, her mother had told her it wouldn't take too long to reach the school once she made it through the portal. Many good things allegedly awaited her. This should be the best time of her life, starting now. So why did it feel like the worst? Using her arms to balance her weight on the railings, she relaxed against them and let the cold air wash over her, calming her racing nerves and burning face.

The ship was even bigger up close. The deck was packed with people, music she couldn't recognize blared from the speakers, and the lights were bright. Excited voices chattered all around her. It was hard not to be overwhelmed by it all. People kept pushing and shoving her out of the way as they moved around her. Whether they were doing it on purpose, she couldn't tell. As she made her way to the main deck, a muffled sound behind her drew her attention. Someone was crying.

As she got closer to the sound, she realized it was a young girl. What was a young girl doing on this ship? Maybe she was someone's little sibling? Or a teacher's child.

"Why are you crying?" she whispered, close to the girl's ears.

The girl stifled another cry and stared up at Ava with bleary eyes. "I miss my daddy!" she wailed, scrunching up her little face. She couldn't have been over ten years old. Why was she here? Surely the school didn't accept students that young.

"I know, it'll be okay. You'll be home soon."

But the girl just wailed louder. Currently, no one was paying them any attention, which Ava hoped would continue until she could get the girl a little calmer, because she was making quite the embarrassing racket.

She also didn't want to have to explain to anyone why this child was crying in front of her. Just what Ava needed was for everyone to think she was the one making her cry.

The girl continued to look around, rocking from side to side. Ava followed her gaze. At the corners of the ship, several other young girls and boys folded into tight groups. Many of them were also crying. Okay, so maybe this was normal. At least no one would accuse her of child abuse. That was good. But she still felt the need to distract this little girl.

"What's your name?" she asked her.

"Priya," the girl mumbled with a distinct English accent as she wiped the snot from her already reddened nose.

"Priya. That's such a pretty name. Where's your daddy now?"

"Over there." The girl pointed down at the throngs of people clustered around the registration counters.

"Okay, you can see him, that's good. Is he coming on the ship with us?"

"Sure, I can see him," the girl responded. "But he's not coming on the ship. So that doesn't help me very much." She sniffled a little more. "He had to get me all registered for my classes." Then the girl's hand flashed across her face and, a second later, Ava was looking at a beautiful bird's wing. Yellow, like a canary.

After another moment, the girl tucked her wing away and flexed her now-human fingers. She explained, "My daddy taught me that trick." She looked proud for a moment, but her expression crumpled once again. "He could've taught me everything I need to know! So why do I have to go to the stupid school, anyway?"

Silently, Ava agreed with her. It was strange to see someone so young at this elite school Ava had previously thought was only for students aged sixteen and above. She was also inwardly jealous this girl had a father who was willing to not only be part of her shifter life, but teach her all these cool things about shifting. Heck, it must be nice to have a father at all!

"Don't say that. You'll see when you get there it'll be a ton of fun, making lots of friends, learning how to master your powers, and I'm sure they will teach you a bunch of cool stuff. You're gonna love it."

"I will?" The girl raised a skeptical eyebrow. "Are you sure about that?"

With her heart pounding 'liar,' Ava nodded emphatically.

"That's what my daddy says, too, but I think he just wants to get rid of me." The girl burst into tears all over again.

"Oh, of course not," Ava tried to reassure her nervously. Then, looking back at the father waving from the registration counter, she could see the concern in his eyes. "Now look, he's worried for you!" She directed Priya's gaze toward her concerned father. "He can tell how sad you are. Can you give him a smile so he can see you're being brave?"

Priya looked up. "They won't even like me; I'm just a canary bird." She made a small C with her thumb and forefinger. "A really tiny canary bird. No one would want to make friends with me."

Ava understood completely where the girl was coming from, and it took everything in her not to say it out loud. Instead, she said, "Absolutely not true! I bet your classmates can't wait to meet you." Ava looked so serious that Priya burst into laughter. Not sure what was so funny, Ava allowed a smile to sneak across her lips. She wished her mother could see this right now. Lucy would find it quite a trip to see Ava consoling a child. Lucy always said Ava was a complete train wreck around kids. Well, look at her now.

Watching the glee in Priya's eyes as her tears dried up, Ava decided to stay with her throughout the rest of the trip. Sure, it might be social suicide, having her introduction to her classmates be seeing her hanging out with a ten-year-old, but she couldn't bring herself to leave the girl. She wondered briefly where her new Miami classmates were, but it didn't matter. They'd gotten away from her the minute they stepped into the registration port. Clearly, she couldn't entertain any fantasies of being friends with them.

"How about we play a game?" Ava spoke at the exact moment the ship's foghorn went off three times and rocked them from side to side. Priya looked very surprised as she had just attempted to stand up but immediately fell into Ava's lap.

"What!?"

Ava repeated herself.

"What game?" The girl sounded intrigued.

"I point at a student, and you make up a story about them." Ava was mildly excited. She used to play a similar game with her mother when they went to the mall together. People-watching was one of Ava's favorites.

"A story? I love stories," Priya squealed.

Ava looked around and searched for the right person. There were all kinds of people around her. Some dressed in more outrageous ways than others. Then she spotted the perfect candidate as the ship fell into a more comfortable groove and sailed smoothly into the sea. "What about that one?"

"That funny dancing boy?"

"Yeah, him." Ava had gestured toward a boy who stood out slightly from the clique about ten feet away from him. He had dyed-black hair, green headphones balanced across his head, and in his lap was a notebook he was presently scrawling on.

"All right," Priya agreed, scrunching her tiny red lips together.

"He's from Asia, probably Japan, and he's running from something or someone..."

"Okay, what else?" Ava prompted.

Priya tapped her cute little chin, her dark eyes narrowed in concentration. "His clothes have not been ironed, his pants are two lengths too short, and they are *way* too tight." She let out a giggle. "His shirt is almost down to his knees; he had to pack and leave in a hurry. He's writing a letter to his family now, to tell them about the crime he committed, and he's on the run, but he's going to be all right."

Ava clapped happily, noticing Priya had completely forgotten to cry for her father as they sailed along. She repressed her smile as best she could and asked again, "Oh yeah? And what about her?" She pointed at a curvy blonde-haired girl looking over the banister of the ship.

"She's heartbroken, clearly."

"Really? And why is that?"

"Look at her. She has stringy hair, like she's been mussing it with her hands, mascara running down her cheeks, and she's not talking to anyone. Her lover must've been someone dangerous. Oh, probably a knight! He had to leave her, against her will, and defend their kingdom."

Ava laughed again. Momentarily, she forgot her own crippling fear of trying to fit in at this new school as she pointed to one person after another. She was having way too much fun with little Priya. Perhaps, with a bit of luck, the academy would be easy for her to survive in after all.

4

The sun had dipped down the horizon. Or something like that. It was at least some sort of fiery red ball, but not like what she was used to in Miami. Although this was under water, so that made sense. According to Priya, the scenery was a magical illusion, put there so the students would feel more comfortable. Ava silently wished she had a magical father to tell her these things like Priya did.

"Do you think we're close?" Priya asked after a while.

"I would think so. We've been sailing for hours at this point."

They had walked around the main deck of the ship somewhat, but still hadn't talked to anyone else. Everyone already seemed to keep to their own cliques.

"I'm hungry," Priya announced, bouncing between her feet. The dark-eyed girl also wore sensible sneakers like Ava did. But hers were beneath a gray skirt that stretched below her knees. A prim and proper princess, her dark blonde hair packed tightly in a bun atop her little head.

"I suppose there's some sort of food around here, right?" Ava asked, more to herself than Priya. "I can go ask around for you, if you like?"

"Okay, I would love that," Priya agreed eagerly. "I'll wait here."

For the first time since the ship had left the tunnel, Ava left Priya on her own and took the opportunity to check out more of the ship. The captain was consulting charts and yelling at others a few feet away. She thought about asking him, but thought better of it because he was probably too busy to talk to a lowly student like her. Looking around for someone else of authority, she felt a tap on her shoulder.

"Are you looking for someone? Maybe I can help."

Ava squinted at the source of the voice. She couldn't make out who it was exactly, because he had stepped toward her and blocked the sun—or the weird fireball or whatever—so she couldn't see his face clearly. But she definitely recognized that unique accent and deep, husky voice.

It was the gorgeous, brown-skinned, white-haired boy from the registration line. She wanted to crawl into herself. But he was smiling at her like he wanted to get to know her.

Just wait until he found out what she was. He would never talk to her again. But, for now, she knew she should make the most of it. *Okay, what the heck, talk to the gorgeous guy.*

She peeked over her shoulder to check on Priya; the girl was laughing and stuffing her face with pie now. Where the heck had she gotten pie so quickly? Oh well, didn't matter now.

Just as she was trying to figure out what to tell the attractive boy she was looking for, since Priya now had pie, the ship lurched and threw Ava forward, directly into the boy's arms.

Her face crashed right into his chest and then —she still couldn't steady herself fast enough— she dropped to her knees at his feet.

"Whoa there!" He laughed loudly, a deep bari-tone sound. "We just met, and I'm pretty sure I should buy you dinner first."

"What?" Ava looked up at him, then realized her face was within an inch of his thighs. "Oh!" She could feel the heat rising to her cheeks. *This may be the worst moment of my life.*

"I'm just messing with you, of course." He stepped back from her and extended his hand.

Trying to will the redness to leave her cheeks, she took his outstretched hand and used him as leverage to pull herself to her feet.

"This is your first year, right?" he questioned her.

Dear God, is it that obvious? Ava wanted to die. Instead, she answered as casually as possible, "Yes, it is," as she tried to brush herself off, but there wasn't anything to brush off—the surrounding area was quite clean.

"Me too!" he announced as he led her around the corner. They were apparently heading up toward a wooden desk, the sound of their footsteps lost in the surrounding noise.

She looked at him, surprised. He was really new? Like her? He seemed so comfortable there. "That's cool."

"Of course, this is a pretty crazy new year for everyone, don't you think?" He placed his fingers gently against her upper arm as he smiled down at her. "Considering they admitted just about anyone, it seems!"

What was he getting at, exactly?

"Oof!" he grumbled suddenly, doubling over.

"Sorry," a high-pitched voice called from some-where. "But watch where you're going." Ava realized it was a young boy who came up to no higher than this guy's waist.

"Even kids." He finally completed his sentence, once again stretching to his full height.

"I don't get it either," Ava admitted. "Do you know why the rules have suddenly changed?"

"No one does. Or at least not anyone I know."

"Really? That's so weird." Ava's heart dropped to her feet. What if she made it all the way to the academy only to be told it was all a mistake, just a terrible error on their part, and she was sent home, rejected and humiliated? Her dream snatched away before it could even begin.

Great, now she would spend the entire year worrying about *that*. Being kicked out. But, on the bright side of all this, that meant there were plenty of others like her: exchange students accepted from all over the world. After all, until this year, this exclusive school formerly accepted only students from Australia unless they were the best of the best. And she was a freaking tabby cat.

Shaking herself out of her thoughts, she returned her attention to what he had just said. "Wait, what do you mean by 'not anyone I know'? If this is your first year, how do you already know people at the school?"

"Oh, I grew up with a few of them. My best friend is actually going here with me this year, but he's sick right now so he will be a few days late. Several other friends of mine are here though."

"You already have shifter friends? Where are you from?" As she asked the question, she was immediately extra curious. She couldn't place his accent at all. He looked Indian, and his accent had an Indian inflection, but that wasn't all.

"I've been living in England with my parents for the past several years," he explained. "My parents moved there from India when I was a kid. There are a lot of shifters there."

So that explained it. His accent was a mix of British and Indian. It actually sounded really cool.

"So, anyway," he went on. "Who or what can I help you find? I got here a lot earlier than everyone else—they deliver from the English branch a lot earlier—so I've had plenty of time to explore the whole ship."

Ava struggled as she searched for something to say. Finally, she just settled on the truth. "I guess I'm not looking for anything anymore. I was going to look for food for my friend, but she figured it out on her own."

"That's cool. Wanna check out the engine room with me then? It's right down there by the kitchen, so we could stop for snacks as backup for your friend or something." He winked adorably.

"Okay, I guess so," she agreed and followed him as he led her down a set of wooden stairs.

"I'm Tarun, by the way. It's nice to meet you." He looked at her over his shoulder as they descended the steps.

"I'm Ava."

"Where you from? Your accent is cute."

Her accent? What was he talking about?

"I'm American. From the Miami branch. What do you mean about my accent? I don't have one."

He started laughing. "To me, you do. And you'll have one to pretty much everyone else here, as well. Except the other Americans, of course. But there aren't that many of you."

She immediately felt stupid. Of course she had an accent. What was she thinking? She promptly changed the subject. "Why the interest in the engine room?"

"I just think it's cool. All those cogs and machines. They fascinate me. I checked it out before the ship even launched." He paused for a moment, twisting his fingers rapidly. Ava feared he might break them.

"Seriously? Why?" She couldn't understand what was so interesting about the ship's engine.

"I don't know. I always wanted to be an engineer. Preferably a mechanical engineer. But then, you know, I manifested. And now..."—He struck a pose as if to say 'Ta-dah!'—"Shifter life. And now I need to be trained for combat."

Ava followed as he resumed walking. She didn't know this guy, but something about his disarming smile and scattered white hair appealed to her. She wondered what kind of shifter he was. Hopefully something embarrassing like her. His eyes were also very catlike—wouldn't it be cool if he were a cat shifter, too? She doubted it though. He seemed way too confident and comfortable there. But hey, a girl could dream.

As they approached a door labeled "Engine Room," Tarun pushed it open to reveal the chaos behind it. The room was enormous, and Ava could see workers dressed in blue overalls. Those close to the flame wore masks that protruded out at least six inches, covering their entire faces. The heat drenched her face in sweat the minute they stepped in. It felt like being thrown in Hell, only hotter.

"Don't worry," Tarun shouted over the roar of the machines. That door must've been soundproof, because she hadn't heard a single thing on the other side of it. "The workers change shifts every fifteen minutes to get some air. Otherwise, they'd suffocate."

Ava nodded. He took her around the room, introduced her to a few of the workers he'd apparently already met, and explained a few parts of the ship she didn't know existed.

"And that's unicorn dust." He pointed to a jar in the corner. It was a relatively tiny glass bottle sitting atop a rough, cracked counter. Ava didn't know when she started walking toward the little canister, but she did. The dust glowed dully in the dying light—a beautiful azure shine.

"What are you doing, come back," Tarun whispered hotly.

She was two steps from it when a worker blocked her way. She paused, coming back to her senses. Something about that dust called out to her—she just wanted to touch it, to run her fingers through it.

"Leave now," the worker said forcefully, as though he could read her thoughts. She jerked back, colliding against Tarun.

"No one is allowed to touch it, Ava, I should've warned you...let's go," he said, dragging her away.

The last thing Ava saw as she left was the worker's glinting eyes. He did not look happy at all.

"What's that used for? I thought unicorns were extinct?"

"They are. But they use it to fire up the ship; that's how we're traveling so fast."

"I see." Although she didn't really. "That was fun," she said as they climbed back up the stairs. Aside from the angry worker, it had been pretty cool after all.

"It really was. Thank you for coming down with me. We could still go back and hit up the kitchen though."

"My friend will be fine," she replied dazedly—the powder was all she could think about. She didn't even notice Tarun walking away when they made it to the deck after several failed tries to talk with her.

It didn't make any sense. Why would they put unicorn dust on display like that when it was the rarest thing to acquire on the planet? Did they have access to one? She could vaguely remember stories her mother told her when she was little...about glorious horned beasts.

A single, tiny shaving off that horn was worth so much. And she knew the ship's crew was abusing it. The powder was supposed to be used for healing, not to fire up boats. Luckily, there wasn't enough time for her to worry...because she looked up and realized the ship had arrived at the shores of Animage Academy.

nimage Academy was known for one thing—and only one thing: churning out the best and most destructive shifters the world had ever seen. The elite. The cream of the crop. The best of the best.

Before this year, the school accepted only with Australia's finest shifters, such as pandas, koalas, kangaroos, wombats, and even sloths. While those particular animals may look cute and cuddly, they were as deadly as could be, especially with training. Exchange students were only brought in from around the world when they were highly coveted. Specifically dragons, wolves, bears, sharks, and birds of prey. They were allowed in even if the student wasn't Australian.

But now? Now it seemed to be a free-for-all.

The academy stood proudly in the light, kissing the clouds, the brown paint across the bricks looking lightly chipped and ancient, but that gave it an even stronger presence. The entire building emitted a strength that came from ages of existence.

Along the sides of the main building stood two trees, as though they were sentinels guarding it. Ava had read in the brochure that they were called Red River Gum trees—native to Australia. Maybe those trees were there for some sort of protection —they certainly looked like it.

About a hundred feet from the front entrance of the main doors, stood a tall and proud oak tree. It was said its leaves represented every student ever admitted in the school. At the base were giant roots that protruded from the earth. No fallen leaves surrounded it. None.

It was heart-wrenching when leaves fell. And they were quickly swept away and buried ceremoniously. Every time a leaf fell from one of those massive branches, it meant one shifter had left the earth realm, crossed over to the other side. In plainer words, died.

It was a scary thought, having her life so closely tied to this tree. There was a magical laser-like barrier around it. Only students of the academy could approach it, and they couldn't tamper with it. A fallen leaf represented the death of a student, and a destroyed leaf meant a destroyed shifter. Ava shuddered at the thought. Scary stuff.

The Animage staff was meticulous about the plant. Ava saw several staff members surrounding it, watering, pruning, and even as she watched, a gardener was trimming back the nearby plants to keep them away from it.

Ava stood ahead of the tree, her jaw literally hanging open in awe. The students had exited the ship without fuss and proceeded down the cobblestone walkway. Whether this magical academy was really underwater, Ava still wasn't sure. It looked like they were outdoors. Beyond the trees, she could see the old building with its own personality. Vines covered many areas. Some windows were long, some were wide, some sheer, and others barred and leaded. It was almost like a patchwork quilt or a jigsaw puzzle put together incorrectly. But somehow, it still looked majestic.

As Paul guided the students down the walkway, he continued to explain all the elements about the school itself. The building was centuries old, but they made additions along the line to suit certain modern requirements. And saying "modern" was a bit of a stretch. Animage was known for its somewhat archaic tendencies. But at least it had indoor plumbing!

Although the bones remained, the additions made it a unique work of art. It appeared to go in all directions, a mass of heights and widths, walls and corners, bricks and boards. There was no symmetry whatsoever. Ava had trouble moving. She simply stood there, overwhelmed and somewhat frightened by the monstrosity. But she could say one thing for sure: she could definitely feel safe inside. It was as sturdy as a rock.

She gulped and decided it was best to hide within the crowd as she entered. That way, they wouldn't pick her out. She clenched her smallest bag close to her, the only one Paul hadn't sent ahead. And they forced her to give up her phone while still on the boat. Cell phones weren't allowed on school grounds for fear the secret would be more likely to leak out to unsuspecting, mundane humans.

As she walked, she kept her eyes fixed on the cobblestones. One foot in front of the other. The path was wide enough to accommodate all the approaching students without excessive shoving. Unconsciously, she kept her hair covering more than half of her face. And as she looked around, she thought to herself that she really should have worn the shoes her mother had picked out for her instead of her sneakers. All the girls passing by her made loud clicking noises with the high heels of their fancy designer shoes.

Beautiful wildflowers lined the pathway. Ava let the scents wash over her. She inhaled deeply, allowing the fragrance to calm her frazzled nerves.

She kept reminding herself there was nothing to fear, nothing to be ashamed of. Not that it helped, because as they got closer and closer, her trepidation spiked. All those doubts came to the surface. She was an embarrassment.

She spotted little Priya ahead. The girl had already made friends with other children her age. Ava smiled sadly. Her only friend so far had already gone off with other children. But that's what children do. She immediately felt ridiculous for feeling jealous of little kids.

It appeared as though the school admitted as many students as possible this year. From all parts of the world. She saw students clad in full burqas, turbans, and kimonos.

The surrounding fragrances grew stronger. No longer floral, but something entirely unique. Ava looked up and sniffed the air. Many shifters have the sharpest of senses. Especially the sense of smell. Instinctively, she knew they were approaching some sort of magical barrier.

She looked down, refusing to lift her head. Her

heart thudded, and she clasped her hands behind her back, noticing they had turned ice cold and somewhat numb. Just a few steps now and she would be inside.

That's when she felt someone lurch into her. She looked up and realized all the students had stopped directly in front of the main steps.

The doors were extremely wide. She saw they were even wider than she initially thought. If she stretched out her arms, she wouldn't be able to reach the doorframe on both sides.

She saw Paul standing ahead of her, right next to the doorway, arranging students into a line on the steps. Had she missed some sort of speech or instructions he had given? The students in front of her were moving ahead and nodding. Was she the only person who didn't know what was happening?

Then she saw the first student approach the doors. A tall red-haired boy clutching a white backpack.

As he entered the doorway, Ava heard a distinct buzzing noise. The school entrance seemed to vibrate, and, immediately, the redhead's human skin fell away in an instant. The gruesome sound of tearing muscles and cracking bones filled Ava's ears.

Squatting in his place in the doorway now was

a cute little black bunny. His pink ears wiggled as he hopped back and forth.

The laughter and the jeers came next.

Oh no.

Apparently the entranceway forced the student to shift....

"Oh look, it's an adorable little bunny!"

Those words may have sounded nice under any other circumstances, but the laughter that followed was just short of brutal.

A nearby attendant, a gorgeous woman dressed in a strict black suit, nodded approvingly, and the bunny hopped in farther, shifting back a moment later, and disappearing inside the building. Thankfully, his clothes shifted with him, otherwise the whole situation would have been ten times more painful.

Well, that was reassuring. At least the school somehow made sure they didn't end up naked for all to see.

Paul continued to guide the students through the entranceway one at a time. Dozens of typical Australian animals went through, as well as a few dragons, a buffalo, two gorillas, several assorted birds, and a handful of some other less-impressive animals. Ava could always tell by the upcoming student's mannerisms if they were about to shift into something they'd rather not. A sheep shifter started shaking uncontrollably and almost fell down the steps twice before he made it to the top. And then a pair of twin guinea-pig shifters were permitted to go through together because one of them wouldn't stop crying.

After that, a group of seven shark shifters went through one by one. Each of them looking around proudly before being forced into their shift. They were particularly interesting to watch because they couldn't walk around. As sharks, they could only lay there and roll around awkwardly before shifting back. The student directly in front of Ava was an octopus shifter. She made an entertaining show of moving up the entranceway wall, sticking herself to the ceiling, shifting back, and doing a graceful and likely well-planned backflip in mid air. She landed with her arms raised and took a bow in front of all the students. Everyone clapped.

Great, thought Ava, *now I have to follow* that.

She took a deep breath as Paul beckoned her forward and gave her a gentle push toward the school entrance.

Here goes nothing. Ava placed one quivering foot on the doorstep, glancing around quickly, hoping most of the students weren't paying her much attention.

Unfortunately, most of them had given their rapt attention to the octopus girl and were still staring intently, waiting to see what Ava would become.

Damn the school security system for this. Perhaps if she'd had time to prepare, she wouldn't be shaking like a leaf in the summer breeze right now. But it made sense the school needed to test every student upon entering. Who knows? Maybe they'd had non-shifter stowaways onboard in the past.

The instant she moved under the archway, that pesky house cat she tried so hard to tamp down in the taxi jumped into existence for all to see. Her clothes vanished, only to return (hopefully) when she morphed back.

The hall on both sides of her erupted in laughter.

She looked around, her ears back in displeasure. Letting out a little meow, she wished she could somehow make them understand this wasn't her fault. It's not like she asked to be a tabby cat.

Her shabby brown fur was the same color of her shabby brown hair, but she had some dark stripes here and there across her whole body. To make matters worse, she was small, even for a cat. When she was younger, she had accidentally shifted in the house a few times and had to run for dear life while Buster chased her around. Even her pug was bigger than she was in her cat form.

The previous name-calling and jeering was nothing compared to what she was currently receiving. Why were they being so mean? Why her? I mean, sure, she was a kitty cat, but the other students hadn't even ridiculed the guinea pigs this badly.

Her ears thumped, and she heard the blood pounding in her head viciously. She couldn't take a second longer, and without waiting for the attendant's approval, her bones elongated, that nauseating cracking noise taking over, and she returned to her human form, her brown hair once again cascading down her back, nearly touching her waist.

Trying not to cry, she popped her nose in the air. *No tears, Ava.* That would be a lot more humiliating.

The attendant shot her a dirty look, but didn't reprimand her for shifting back too early. Instead, she pointed toward a desk behind her where several students waited in line to receive their room allocation.

Upon receiving her room number, she barely looked at what was written on it, and hightailed it out of there as quickly as possible. She didn't know where she was going, even though there were attendants everywhere trying to give directions, but it seemed the majority of the students lining the halls were headed in one direction, so she followed suit.

Eventually, she was able to get her wits about her enough to look at the room allocation on the card she was holding. She expected a series of numbers, but the only thing printed on the maroon card was the number three. She flipped it over a couple more times before looking up with a confused expression.

That couldn't be right. Just number three? She looked closer at other students passing by—they were holding cards like hers, but the cards were different colors. Did that mean something? She should've paid better attention.

She looked around, somewhat frantically, for another school attendant who could help her. That's when she noticed a group of beautiful but not-at-all-friendly-looking girls push past her, holding maroon cards as well. One of them shot her an unpleasant side glance, and then said, just loud enough for Ava to hear, "Oh goody, they put the tiny kitten in Maroon with us."

Ava groaned. What did they mean by tiny kitten? She was a full-grown tabby, darn it. Just wait, she would scratch those mean girls' eyes out one by one. She would show them who looked harmless and cute.

Still reeling from the whole ordeal in the

entranceway, and the girls' comments, it took her a minute to notice the maroon doorway and the gleaming curved stairs that whirled beneath it where all those girls holding the maroon cards had disappeared.

Wait a second, they said the academy put me in Maroon... That must be the name of the dormitory wing....

Still seething relentlessly, she jogged after them, completely unaware of the other stir her presence was causing nearby.

6

Tarun stood next to Deacon, a gorilla shifter, on the adjacent stairway. Their attendant was spouting instructions and the rules of the dormitories, but neither of them were paying much attention. Deacon was the first to spot her. "Yo! Dude, check out that hot little thing over there."

Tarun slapped his friend lightly upside the head. "Stupid comments like that are why you're still single." But even so, he followed Deacon's gaze and recognized her instantly. The pretty girl he had shown around on the boat. The one who had almost knocked him off his feet, both literally and figuratively.

"Too bad she's a house cat. Can't be seen with

her." Deacon was just rambling at that point, and Tarun was trying to ignore him.

"Although even if we can't hang around together in public, I wouldn't mind getting her behind closed doors..." Deacon just kept on going.

That got Tarun's attention. "Dude, what the heck is wrong with you? You seriously wouldn't hang out with that super-hot girl just because she's a tabby cat?" A look of disgust crossed over his features. "But you would still be happy to have your way with her as long as no one knew?"

Deacon didn't seem to notice the horror crossing Tarun's features. "No, of course not. She would never fit in with us."

Tarun didn't answer. He was too busy staring at Ava. He watched her lick her lips and take a swipe at her eyes. Was she crying?

"You're stupid, Deacon," he finally said. But Deacon just kept plowing forward like a bulldozer. "Now that chick right there—*her* I would be happy to show off."

Tarun looked around. "Which one?"

"Blonde hair, huge boobs, pink low-cut shirt. Right that way." He pointed.

"Oh, yeah, I see her." Tarun sounded little more than mildly interested. "What is she?"

"Is your eyesight going, old man?" Deacon teased. "You can't see that shifter mark? From the looks of it, she's some sort of bird of prey. Looks like an eagle or a falcon."

Tarun just glared daggers at Deacon before pulling his head back toward their dormitory attendant giving instructions.

The big-chested blonde girl didn't look like an agreeable person. Tarun could tell she was being rude to those near her. "It looks like she's practically punching people out of the way. Doesn't that bother you?"

Deacon just chuckled. "She's a fiery one, that's all." He was still twisting his head backward to get a good look at her when their group reached the top of their stairs.

"Didn't we meet her at the school tour this summer?" Tarun asked.

"Oh, that's right! Eagle shifter for sure. What was her name?"

Tarun shook his head. He didn't remember, and he didn't want to.

Following a group of students, Ava finally found an attendant to explain where she needed to go. Ava stopped at the second door on her left...at the top of the Maroon stairs, and stared at the sign on it. Number three. This was it. She slid the old-fashioned gold key they gave her into the lock and turned it until it clicked open.

"Dinner's at six, don't be late," the attendant called out from down the hallway.

She certainly wouldn't be, and her stomach rumbled in agreement.

As soon as she stepped inside the room, she froze where she was.

It looked like someone had vomited Pepto Bismol all over the interior of the room. Everything was bright pink. Well, half of it anyway. The bed, pillows, walls, table, even the ceiling was pink with glitter. Yes, glitter. Ava suppressed a tiny gag.

She was still standing there with a look somewhere between confusion and disgust across her face when a pretty blonde girl exited the bathroom, snapping a makeup compact shut. The girl was halfway to her pink bed before she noticed Ava standing in the doorway.

"Who are you?" the girl asked. Her skin sparkled everywhere it was exposed from her strapless pink top. Had she seriously covered *herself* in glitter? And how was she breathing in that tight thing she was wearing?

Ava couldn't read the girl's expression, but she guessed the girl was less than thrilled to see her. "I... Uh... I'm Ava. Ava Carrington."

The girl's perfectly drawn-on right eyebrow slid up her forehead.

This was clearly someone who was aware of her power and used to using it, Ava noted, her heart sinking. She'd really been hoping for a roommate she could get along with. Then at least she would have one friend.

"And what is that supposed to mean to me?" asked the girl, finally.

"Well, I'm your new roommate," Ava confirmed, even though she thought it should have been obvious. She observed the girl further. She would've been truly stunning if it weren't for the perpetual sneer on her lips. Her eyes were also entirely too narrow.

The girl rolled her eyes. "Ugh, I told Marta I was fine on my own!" Whoever Marta was, Ava didn't want to be in her shoes. This sassy blonde looked ready to kill.

"Well, it's already done, so which bed is mine?" Ava asked and immediately regretted it. It was pretty obvious which one was hers. The one that didn't look like it was set in Barbie's pink palace.

The girl drew the back of her hand to her hairline and rolled her eyes toward the ceiling, grumbling, "Please, not a stupid one."

For the umpteenth time today, Ava wanted to crawl into a hole and die. "Right, I'll take that one."

And she moved toward the second bed. Thankfully, the beds were pretty far apart from each other. Their room was quite sizable.

"I assume these are yours?" The girl pulled open the closet Ava hadn't seen until just now because it was so pink it blended in with everything else.

"Oh, yes, my bags." Ava didn't know how Paul had pulled that off, but she shook her head and moved to grab them gratefully. It was his job, after all. But she would worry about that later, because, for now, she had a pissed-off queen bee on her hands.

"You haven't told me your name..." Ava ventured, trying to see if she could make the best of this conversation. Maybe, once the girl realized having a roommate was inevitable, they could be friends. That's what roommates did, right? Learned to love each other?

The girl walked toward her slowly, her hips swinging from left to right. When she was inches from Ava's face, she jabbed her perfectly manicured pink pointy fingernail into Ava's chest. "I'm Elaine. Never, ever, touch my stuff."

Ava stared back at her. *Okay, maybe not then.*

7

Tarun leaned against the wall, watching.

His bowtie was choking him, and he readjusted it for the fifth time in probably two minutes.

He'd somehow managed to get his errant strands of white hair to relax against his scalp; despite that, he compulsively smoothed it back over and over. Occasionally, he sipped his drink, more for something to do than because he was actually enjoying it. It was just some sour nonalcoholic wine the school opted to serve instead of the real thing.

Soft music filled the atmosphere, spilling over from the orchestra on the stage. Couples swirled past him, pretty gowns twinkling and shoes shining. The atmosphere reminded him of the ballroom scenes in the movie *Titanic*. And he felt just as ridiculous and out of place as Jack. He remained in the dark, somewhat shaded part of the hallway, not ready to do much socializing.

Well, unless *she* came around. He would be interested in socializing with *her*, for sure. He checked his watch in the dim light. The gathering had started thirty minutes earlier. This was a bit beyond fashionably late. Where was she anyway?

There she is.

Dressed in a shimmering gold floor-length gown, so stunning he could almost mistake her for a model, Ava stood by the door.

His eyes followed the movement of her fingers as they trailed up and down her naked arms. She was rubbing them as if she was cold or uncomfortable or both. At the sight of her, his mouth went dry.

Shaking himself out of his stupor, he gulped down the rest of the drink, slurping it much more noisily than intended, and almost spilled it down the front of his pristine white shirt. He moved to set down his glass so he could go greet her.

"Tarun."

He turned to look for the source of the voice.

"That's your name, right?"

Before him stood the attractive yet unpleasant blonde Deacon had been ogling earlier.

"Yes, that's right." He tried to glance at her name tag without staring too intently at her chest. "And you are Elaine?"

"Yes, that's right. I think we met on the school tour over the summer." She shot him a seductive smile and then angled her shoulder forward— pushing up her cleavage even more—so he could get a good look at her right arm. She pointed to her shifter mark there. "I'm an eagle shifter. Fifteen- foot wingspan, I might add." She winked at him. "How about you?"

"Bengal tiger," he murmured into his glass as he tried to take another sip before remembering it was empty. He cleared his throat awkwardly and lowered the glass back down, hoping she hadn't noticed his faux pas. "I remember you from the tour now. You're American, right?"

"Sure am." Elaine giggled at him, probably assuming his awkwardness was because he was attracted to her. "California girl."

Great.

"What do you think of my dress?" She changed the subject and did a slow twirl, making an effort to pop out her chest and backside a little extra as she turned. "Too much?"

Instead of telling her what he was thinking, which was that she looked like a plastic Barbie doll in that ridiculous pink dress, he said, "You look stunning."

She covered her mouth and giggled, her exposed shoulders quaking with the effort, making everything else jiggle. "I know, right?"

Tarun refrained from rolling his eyes. Was this girl for real?

"Oh! Come with me and try these pastries, I promise, they taste like you're biting into Heaven." Without waiting for acquiescence, she grabbed his bicep and pulled him along behind her. He couldn't even get a word in as she dragged him away. He made a last-ditch effort to look around for Ava who was barely visible edging her way toward the other wallflowers. Hopefully, he would get a chance to talk to her later.

Ava watched Elaine drag Tarun across the hall. It figured they would be interested in each other— they were both gorgeous, after all. Ava let out a little sigh and fought disappointment. And it had turned out maybe Elaine was a decent person after all, so she shouldn't be bothered. Even though Elaine had been rude to her initially, she'd ended up rescuing Ava from a social disaster, for which Ava would remain forever grateful.

After their initial unpleasant encounter, Elaine had ignored Ava completely until she was ready to go to dinner, hogging the bathroom the entire time so Ava couldn't even get in there.

When Ava was heading for the door, dressed in her blue jeans and button-down shirt and sneakers, as usual, Elaine had stopped her by grabbing her shoulder and jerking her backward.

Ava stopped and gaped at Elaine, who was dressed in a ridiculous bubblegum pink floor-length evening dress. Initially, Ava possessed an impulse to slam the door on the pretty blonde's face, but the determination in Elaine's eyes made Ava pause and listen.

"Where do you think you're going?" Elaine questioned her accusingly.

"To dinner, obviously." She'd resisted a powerful urge to roll her eyes.

Elaine chuckled. "Dressed like that? I can't let you do that. They will eat you alive."

"Why? What's wrong with what I'm wearing? We aren't supposed to be in our uniforms or anything, are we?" Ava realized that perhaps she should have paid better attention to the stack of brochures the attendant had handed her when she first got there. It appeared Elaine knew something she didn't, which was probably why Elaine was dressed like that. Was this supposed to be formal?

"For starters, everything." Elaine dropped the fashion magazine she'd been holding and circled Ava until it got uncomfortable. "And no, definitely no uniforms. Are you kidding me?" She gestured to her own ensemble, her perfectly lined lip curling up. "Was my outfit not enough of a clue for you? As your roommate, I guess I'm responsible for making sure you look presentable tonight."

And that was how Ava ended up wearing the beautiful gold gown with matching high heels. Her mother had bought her the shoes the previous Christmas, but she never intended to wear them. She didn't even realize her mother had snuck them in her suitcase! And, thankfully, Elaine turned out to have a perfectly matching dress for her.

After tossing the dress at Ava, Elaine had left her to her own devices to get ready, which was why Ava ended up thirty minutes late, and now she was starving. Shifting always took a lot out of her, and she hadn't eaten a thing since she left her apartment.

"So when does dinner actually start? Do you know?" Ava asked the girl closest to her, tapping her lightly on the shoulder from behind.

The girl swiveled around, and Ava's eyes widened slightly. Had Ava been attracted to women, she would've been smitten. This girl was stunning. Her bare skin looked like literal chocolate. Deep brown and glossy. Her hair was short and curly, held up with several pins, and big yellow hoops hanging from her ears caught the light and twinkled as the girl moved her head.

"I don't know yet, but I've been standing right here since I arrived, and these shoes are killing me!" She spoke with a thick African accent, slowly, probably so people could understand her.

"Oh, that sucks. I'm really famished," Ava complained, "I haven't eaten since breakfast."

"I hear you, and after that stupid security check at the entrance, I feel like I'm going to pass out from starvation," the girl scoffed.

"You too? I thought it was just me. My mom is always on me about eating like a lady, but shifting just takes so much energy!"

"Especially when it's been a while, right?"

"Yes, exactly!" An easy smile creased her lips. "I'm Ava."

"Winta." The girl extended her hand.

Ava took it quickly, realizing it had probably seemed rude that she hadn't offered hers first when she introduced herself. "That's a really beautiful name." She meant it, too; the name suited the owner perfectly. Elegant and mysterious.

"Thank you. It means desire." She shrugged.

"It's kind of awkward to have that name." Her voice was soft with a lilt and a slight lisp at the end of each sentence.

"Well, it's still beautiful." Ava offered her a smile. Then, changing the subject, "So, Winta, why aren't you dancing? You could take off your shoes like some of those other girls did." She pointed.

A shadow crossed Winta's face, her round and full features pinching up a little. Her nostrils flared slightly. "I don't want to," she said flatly. Her lashes swept down, shading her eyes from Ava's view.

Not that Ava was one to talk; she wasn't dancing either; despite that, she said, "I mean, it seems like it could be fun."

"Are you asking me to dance with you?" Winta raised an eyebrow and laughed.

"Oh! No, I—"

But it was too late. Winta grabbed Ava's hand, and together they crossed to the dance floor. Winta took the lead because she was the taller of the two.

Winta rolled her eyes playfully. "You just couldn't let me enjoy my peace over there as a happy wallflower, could you?" she teased.

Ava let out a genuine laugh. She didn't expect this, but she was having a good time. Then the music sped up to a fast waltz, and that shut her up real quick.

Apparently Winta knew what she was doing on

the dance floor, and Ava could barely keep up with her. They whirled around together, laughing, completely disregarding the fact half the room avoided them like the plague, probably for fear of being stepped on.

"Admit it, you're having fun!" Ava screamed over the music.

"A teeny bit," Winta huffed. "Perhaps."

A tingling bell rang through the room, drawing their dizzy eyes to the podium. The music faded and the commotion around the girls died down.

Ava looked around the room. She noticed most of the original Aussies were sticking to their own. Because of the formal attire for the night, it was easy to see what most of the females shifted into because their arms were exposed. The boys, however, were all wearing suits or tuxedos, so there was no way to see any of their shifter marks.

Ava could make out a group of dolphin girls nearby sticking together. They were all giggling and cackling. Made sense, they really sounded like dolphins.

There were other clusters of students around, too. Some were a mix of both boys and girls. Based on the marks on the girls' arms, Ava knew they were shifters she wouldn't want to mess with. There was a group of seven dragons. She also recognized a bear shifter, some sort of lion, and a gorilla mark in a group of at least a dozen. Ava guessed they were all predators. Tarun stood close to them. So much for her wish that he was a cat like her. That meant he was probably some sort of predator, too. She wondered what kind.

Nearby, Elaine stood by her group of girls, all birds of prey, and a pack of wolves hovered behind them.

Sheesh. Some of these shifters were terrifying.

Scattered around the cliques were, well, everyone else. Ava could make out the guinea-pig twins hovering toward the back, girls with bunny marks, and a few sheep.

An older woman, silver-haired, pencil thin, and eagle-eyed, but still beautiful, rang the gold bell again and brought the room down to complete silence.

"Welcome to Animage Academy." The woman held out her arms as if waiting for a hug. "For those of you who are new here, I am Headmistress Levine. As you may have noticed, we make comfort a priority for the four years you will spend with us. You will lack nothing, but..."

Several shifters groaned.

"But..." the woman continued, raising her deep voice a tad more. "We still do not provide you with modern conveniences. We keep the academy old-fashioned in many ways. And we do this for several reasons. There will be no electronic communication."

More groans from the crowd.

"Students from last year, we are aware of the changes, and we expect you to cooperate with the new shifters. There are no exceptions. We expect genuine camaraderie at the school. Your obligation is to embrace one another as your own, even with the influx in foreign-exchange students." She hesitated. "It is unnecessary to avoid fellow shifters as I see most of you doing right now."

Slight murmuring filled the room, but no one moved to cover the gaps.

Levine let out a sigh. "I see we have our work cut out for us. For now, enjoy your party and welcome to Animage Academy!"

The spattering of clapping noises turned to halfhearted applause before everyone proceeded through an enormous set of double doors into the next room.

"I still can't believe this," Ava said from the side of her mouth to Winta. Ava had been referring to the fact she'd been accepted to the school. But Winta didn't seem to take it that way.

"Yeah, it looks just like my father's dining room!" Winta cried out as she clapped her hands. Her eyes wide as she gazed at the tables full of food.

Ava looked up and gasped. And here she thought the ballroom was extravagant, but the dining hall was even more impressive. Tables extended across the room with more food than Ava could ever have dreamed up.

Wait, what?

"Did you just say this looks like your father's dining room?" Ava looked at Winta. "Are you telling me his dining room has—let me count—three, no, *four* chandeliers hanging from the ceiling? And tables filled with hundreds of special foods? More than any of us would even be able to finish?"

Winta's lips quirked; a lopsided grin took over her face that was both endearing and condescending. "Usually, yes."

"Usually?"

"Yes, but sometimes, if we have company, he likes to be more extravagant."

Ava just blinked. "Is he like...a king or something?"

"Or something," Winta answered quietly, piquing Ava's curiosity further.

But that's when Ava spotted her name on a place card three chairs away from the headmistress. "Oh, that's me." Her focus moved to filling her stomach and away from Winta's rich father.

She pulled out the chair, a high-backed

wooden chair covered in red velvet.

"Oh, and it looks like this is me!" Winta squealed, pointing to a seat across the table from Ava, only a few chairs down.

Headmistress Levine, who already sat at the head of the table, glared at Winta.

"Sorry," Winta mumbled, as she made her way to her chair, but she winked at Ava. Then Winta rushed to get seated, clasped her hands on her lap, her back ramrod straight, looking straight ahead. As prim and proper as could be.

Headmistress Levine harrumphed and looked away, relaxing her pencil-thin eyebrows. Her attention quickly moved to the boy seated directly next to her, who reached across her to grab heaping spoonfuls of the food, barely sparing her a glance. The headmistress rolled her eyes.

Throughout the meal, Levine explained that the students were seated according to seniority. The first-year students sat closest to the headmistress. Although the young children had their own separate dining room and welcome party. A new wing was built in the school especially for them because the academy had never allowed children under sixteen before now.

Ava briefly wondered how Priya was doing as she hadn't seen her since entering the building.

Shoving chicken into her mouth, Ava tried to

drown out her insecurities. Exposing her shifter mark didn't matter now because everyone at the school had already seen what she was. And even if they hadn't, word would spread fast.

But, on the bright side, she had a new best friend, hopefully. Although, now that she thought about it, she didn't even know what Winta shifted into.

She snuck a glance across the table to where Winta was delicately pulling tomatoes out of her salad with her fork. The pretty yellow dress Winta wore had puffy sleeves that hung over her arms. Ava wondered if Winta was purposely trying to cover her mark. The tip of Winta's mark peeked above her right sleeve, but Ava couldn't make out what animal it was.

Ava supposed that wasn't important. Winta liked her, and that was all that mattered.

Another thought nagged at her as she assaulted her food. The saltshaker reminded her of the unicorn powder she'd seen on the ship. What was with that? Once she got a little more settled, maybe she would do some digging. Not that it was any of her business, but it called out to her for some reason.

Unicorns were extinct, so the dust would be super rare. Yet the powder was being used liberally just for transport? It didn't add up.

8

Winta and Ava trailed behind the other students in clusters back to the dorms. Everywhere Ava looked, she saw fancier dresses, fancier shoes, fancier hairstyles. These shifters weren't playing.

The girl right beside her took the cake, easily and absolutely. Her jewelry alone could pay rent on Ava's apartment back home for at least a year. *Good lord.*

Looking at all the stunning riches around her, Ava remembered Winta's comment about the dining hall earlier. "You still haven't told me about your father."

Winta chuckled, showing off her tiny chiseled white teeth. "Dad? Oh, there's not much to tell.

He's a businessman." She hesitated. "Among other things."

"Other things like what?" For whatever reason, Ava was super curious—a cat thing.

"Well, he's a shifter. One like me. I'm sure he's the reason I got into this school."

"You mean you think he got you into the school because of his money, or because he's a shifter? Because I don't know if you've noticed, but we are *all* shifters here!" Ava then fell silent, unwilling to push Winta into revealing what she didn't want to. Even though her raging curiosity was getting the better of her. But her mother always reminded her...

Curiosity killed the cat, right?

Winta didn't seem terribly put off. "I just mean because of the kind of shifter he is. He's powerful. My entire family is." And she left it at that only to move on. "What about you?"

"What do you mean?" Ava looked up at her. Their height difference was significant, even though Ava was wearing taller heels. "What about me?"

"Your family—are they all shifters? Or just your father? It's my understanding that the shifting gene is usually passed down on the male side."

"Oh, I don't really know. He...um... He left before I was born, so..."

"He just left you? That's awful. I'm so sorry. I suppose that's even worse than dying."

Ava glared at her.

"Sorry, I just mean, well, when a parent dies, you know it's not their fault. For you, your dad just left you. And that's really horrible." She gritted her teeth. "So again, I'm sorry. I spoke out of turn. I shouldn't have said that."

Ava loosened her shoulders. "It's okay, I mean, you're right, anyway." Then she went on. "But my mom's a tabby cat, too. So I'm guessing that's what he was as well. Honestly, I've never even known if he was also a shifter or not, but since you just said it's passed down on the father's side, I guess that means he was also a tabby cat?"

"Yeah, more than likely." Then Winta scrunched her brow as if she thought of something. "Why don't you just ask your mom?"

Ava let out a loud guffaw. "You don't think I've tried? Believe me, I've brought it up way more than she would like. But she never talks about him, and she just won't. One time, I pressed her a little too much, and, well, I won't do that again."

"Oh?" Winta queried, dragging her dress down for the umpteenth time.

"Let's just say there is still a spaghetti stain on the kitchen wall right above where I sit at the table, and we now have an odd number of matching dinner plates." Ava chuckled at the memory, even though it really wasn't a laughing matter at the time.

Apparently Winta didn't know what to say to that because she didn't respond.

Awkwardly, Ava traced the patterns on the wall with her fingers. They had stopped at the base of the Maroon stairs. "It's just, you know, it's heartbreaking to watch your mother melt down like that."

Winta, probably sensing the pain behind Ava's nonchalant words, rested her hand over her slim waist. I'm sure he had a good reason for leaving—"

Ava's chin jerked up, nostrils flaring. "What reason could he possibly have for choosing to leave his pregnant wife?" She didn't give Winta a chance to answer. "I will tell you. None! Definitely none. Only a terrible father and a coward would do such a thing."

Then, she stepped forward and jabbed her finger into Winta's chest with each word: "Don't. Make. Excuses. For. Him."

Winta couldn't say the words fast enough. "Okay! Okay, I get it. You're right."

Ava took a deep breath and said nothing.

Winta, opting to diffuse the tension, said, "Come on, don't let him ruin this night, too." She reached down and cupped Ava's shoulder, shaking her slightly. "Hey, what about that boy in there who couldn't take his eyes off you?"

Ava grew animated in nanoseconds. "What? Where?"

Winta laughed jovially. "The muscular Indian boy with the white hair."

"You mean Tarun!?" Ava practically squawked. "There's no way."

"Oh, there was definitely a way. I caught him quite a few times. And he blushed and looked away every time I made eye contact with him."

Ava just shook her head and rolled her eyes playfully. "Whatever." She tried to act as nonchalant as possible, but, admittedly, her heart was pounding a little faster. Could there be any truth to it?

Ava took a couple steps up the Maroon staircase, then looked back at Winta. "Oh, I'm sorry, I didn't even think about it. Where is your room? I guess it's not in Maroon?"

Winta shuffled her feet uncomfortably. "No, it's back that way. Indigo Dorm."

"Oh, okay. I'll walk you over there." She wasn't necessarily eager to see Winta's room, but she was eager to spend more time with her so she could avoid going back to her own room with the cranky queen bee.

But Winta shook her head. "No, I don't want to do that."

"Why? Do you not like your roommate?"

"I don't have a roommate."

"Really? Did your father make sure of that or something? I thought we all had to have roommates our first year for sure."

"What? No. I'm just..." Winta bit her bulbous bottom lip. "I'm too big, okay?"

Ava angled her head. Yeah, sure, Winta wasn't exactly petite, but what did she mean by... Oh, wait... "You still shift in your sleep, too?"

The shadow that had crossed Winta's face when Ava asked her to dance earlier was back, but even darker this time. "I shift into an elephant, all right?" she grumbled. "A really gigantic elephant. It runs in my family. My father is the size of a house." Headmistress Levine worried I might suffocate my roommate or something, so she suggested I stay alone until I learn to control my shifting."

Ava knew her eyes were wide in astonishment, but she didn't want her new friend to feel more uncomfortable than she already did. She wanted to reach out, to hug her, to reassure her it wasn't her fault. Because Ava definitely understood her pain. What it felt like—the embarrassment of what she was. And suddenly all her worries about not fitting in dimmed at Winta's issue. Here Ava was worried about being bullied for being helpless and small, but Winta had the opposite problem. "Wait, so what happens if you shift in your sleep and accidentally crush the furniture?" Ava had to know. It was very common for younger shifters to shift in their sleep or when they got overly stressed, like Ava almost did in the Uber ride in Miami. But Ava never considered how inconvenient it would be if she were a bigger animal.

Winta groaned. "I keep my belongings in a room over in the Indigo wing—a room that *is* actually shared with someone—but that's not where I sleep. I..." She rolled her eyes upward. "I sleep outside. In the back courtyard."

"Oh, my gosh!" Ava's hand flew over her mouth. "Are you serious? They make you sleep outside?"

"Well, yeah. It's not like they have a choice. Back home, my parents had to do the same thing with me. And my two older brothers had to sleep outside until they were old enough to control their abilities as well."

It made sense, Ava supposed, but it still sounded pretty awful. "How long did it take for them to get enough control to keep that from happening?"

"Both of them could sleep inside again by their third year here."

"So you're telling me you might be stuck sleeping outside for at least two years?" Ava wasn't even bothering to hide her shock at this point.

Winta just shrugged. "Could be worse."

Ava then latched on to something Winta had said. "So your brothers went here too then? The academy accepted them even though they were from Africa?"

"Yes." Winta nodded. "Elephant shifters are very rare, and very powerful. Animage likes powerful shifters, so they accepted them as foreign exchange students. My parents were students here as well."

"Wow," Ava whispered. "So really, it was no surprise to you when you got your acceptance letter. You knew you were coming here all along."

"That's right."

Briefly, Ava wondered what it was like to come from a family of powerful shifters. And what had possessed Winta to befriend her. Her shifter mark had been on full display the whole evening, so Winta knew exactly what she was as soon as they met. But she still wanted to be her friend. Maybe just because Winta also knew what it was like to feel awkward in her own skin. Right then, Ava knew she had found a true friend within the academy. And if they couldn't fit in, at least they'd stand out together.

9

"I magine it. Focus on that image. Let it be the focal point of all your thoughts. Let it clutch your heart and release your soul. Envision it. Can you see?" Sir Waters called out to his class.

There were a few mutterings and nothing more. They'd been at this all day, and it seemed like they were getting nowhere.

Sir Waters was an English knight—rumor had it he once saved the queen's life, though no one had confirmed it—the only one in the school. Also, the oldest—a tortoise shifter. He always dressed impeccably in a full suit for every class. Sir Waters spoke the Queen's English alone and considered all who couldn't absolute imbeciles. For now, he had the first-years to deal with, and he wasn't having a great time of it.

This was the third time he had tried to show them the simple act of transformation by acting exactly like the animal they embodied. So far, he'd had conversations with an eagle, a raven, and a bear, but none of them transformed.

The issue was, for the students anyway, that none of those animals could talk. So his students kept failing. They hadn't yet mastered the ability to transform only certain body parts, like vocal cords. Of course, Sir Waters would know that, but he was certainly acting like he didn't.

"Don't just transform, *become* the animal! See through their eyes. Hear like them. Feel like them. If your second form eats grass, then you bloody well eat grass, too!"

This was just getting downright painful.

He stopped, dark sunken eyes almost popping out of their sockets. Unsteadily, he limped from the teacher's podium—he had taken a sword to the thigh and had a peg leg—to get closer to what he believed to be the poorest, dumbest class in the academy's history. Damn new policy. If he'd had his way, none of them would be here.

Sir Waters waved his walking cane at a girl in the corner. The same girl Ava had met from the Miami branch. The rather unpleasant pink-haired girl. Michaela. Turned out she was a first-year, too, so that made her snotty comment about Ava's bags the first day they met *extra* rude.

The girl froze mid-sentence of a hot whisper.

"You there! Pink Hair! Step out, please."

"Me?" Michaela asked, prodding at her chest.

"Unless there's another ridiculous pink-haired lass here, step out!"

There were plenty of other pink-haired students, actually, but she was the only one in the nearby vicinity. She looked back at her friends where they huddled next to the wall, her eyes pleading for help. No one made a move. She was on her own. Everybody knew when Sir Waters called a shifter out, it usually ended in tears.

"Stand right there."

When she moved to do what he asked, he bellowed at her, "Now!"

Michaela jumped and tripped over her own feet.

Sir Waters brought his palm to his forehead. "And what exactly would you say knocked you down, huh?" Then he pulled his hand away and waved it as if he were shooing a fly. "Never mind, don't answer that." He limped closer to her. "Just get over here. Stand where the light of the sun can touch you."

"Y—yes— sir."

"Finally!" He readjusted his dark shades and scanned the class for another victim. "Good, good."

Everyone in the classroom froze, perhaps hoping his vision couldn't detect movement, and he wouldn't see them as long as they held still. "I want to teach you, but you refuse to learn. Do you know how I do this?" He tapped the sides of his shades with his cane. "I'm a bloody blind teacher who can see every single one of you! Can someone attempt to tell me why that is?"

A brave boy spoke up. "You use your other eyes, Sir. Your second form."

Sir Waters twisted to see the courageous—or perhaps insolent—soul who volunteered to answer his mind-numbingly simple question. "And you are...?"

"Gregory." At Sir Waters' raised puckered lips, and creased bushy eyebrows, he rushed to add, "Sir."

Sir Waters used his cane to beckon Gregory to join Michaela in the sun. His cane making tap-tap noises on the hardwood floor as he walked around them, as if just waiting for someone to breathe wrong.

"Once you become the master of your animal, you can control parts of your body without transforming fully." He hobbled up to Gregory, his newest victim.

"All right then, Gregory, would you mind standing a little closer to the lady?"

Gregory started to grumble, but caught himself. Unfortunately, Waters missed nothing in his class.

"Did I just hear a complaint?"

Gregory went rigid as a board, his eyes as wide as saucers. "No, Sir!"

"Good, I thought not. Now, stand right there and join hands."

Gregory and Michaela did what they were told.

Trying to show off that she already knew what she was doing somewhat, Michaela shifted a bit, almost imperceptibly, but of course, Waters noticed and glared at her.

"Wait until I give you the go-ahead! So help me God, young madam, I will fail you just because you irk me."

Michaela just cleared her throat and stood a little straighter.

Sir Waters went on, "Concentrate on the area you want to shift—imagine it is already part of you, whatever it is you're shifting into... Now, hold his hand tighter, make eye contact, and try to catch the rays of sun with your joined hands. Relax, focus, and allow it to happen. This is the easiest time you will ever have with this because the rays of the sun bring forth your abilities, and you are holding hands with another shifter and utilizing each other's power, so to speak."

He looked around the room again. "Did you all catch that?" He tapped his temple.

The class nodded.

"So now learn to master it! Are you ready?" He was speaking to Michaela and Gregory this time.

They both nodded vigorously and then squeezed their eyes shut.

"Proceed," Waters said calmly.

Slowly, the two shifters' bodies began to morph as the words left his mouth.

Michaela's back hunched, and hair sprouted across her arms.

Gregory didn't get any shorter, but he definitely got wider. Their hands remained tightly clasped until the last possible second when they could no longer hold their paws.

They stared at each other amid claps from all their mates. Michaela, a beautiful gray and white wolf; Gregory, a fluffy black and white panda, the circles covering his tiny dark, luminescent eyes.

"What in the bloody hell happened?" Sir Waters waved his cane in the air. "You weren't supposed to shift all the way! You knew that! I know you knew that! Especially you, Pink Hair!"

Michaela turned and bared her teeth, letting out a terrifying growl.

He whopped her on the head with his cane, and she whimpered. "None of that now! Now let's do this right."

Michaela sat back on her haunches and then let out a howl.

Sir Waters leaned forward expectantly.

Soon, the piercing sound of the wolf's howl changed to a lower-pitched human voice—almost like a yodel. Then, her howl stopped, and she spoke in her normal human voice, if not perhaps with a bit more of a guttural tone: "There, are you happy now, *Sir*?" The inflection of the last word was as snide as could be, but Sir Waters didn't miss a beat.

"Actually, yes!" Sir Waters clapped his hands. "Very much so!"

Turning his attention to the panda next, and tapping him aside the head, he said, "Now, you!"

Gregory struggled with it more than Michaela had, but eventually, he figured it out.

"Wonderful!" Sir Waters praised them both.

Then, turning back to the class, he paired them all off to try the same thing.

After many comical attempts, and a couple of shifting mishaps by the less experienced, the cacophony of animal noises filled his ears from all sides.

Finally, Sir Waters noticed a girl who'd been standing alone in the back of the class. She was pale and lanky, with her arms folded into each other. She seemed uncomfortable there. She was a pretty little thing, but would have definitely been prettier with more confidence, instead of hiding behind her mousy brown hair like that. The pink, yellow, and black plaid uniform dress hung on her curveless body in an unflattering way, and her plain high-top sneakers didn't help, but as soon as she looked up at him with her catlike eyes, he recognized her immediately.

"Ava Carrington... We finally meet."

Ava had been studiously avoiding the teacher's eyes the entire class, but that aside, how in the world did he know her name? They weren't wearing name tags and there was nothing distinct about her. And she was wearing the same uniform as all the other girls, for crying out loud!

"Yes, Sir?" she responded, her voice little more than a whisper. She did her best to hold her chin up, and then she stepped forward into the light streaming in from the window, casting a hazy glow around her. It was as if the light was attracted to her, kissing her skin.

"Stay where you are!" the professor instructed.

Ava didn't argue. This man was terrifying.

The man pointed his cane at her. "Now shift."

Ava remained exactly as she was. There was no way in hell he was going to convince her to transform in front of everyone so they could ridicule her. It didn't matter that Sir Waters looked ready to murder her. She wasn't moving a single bone.

"Did I stutter?" he questioned her in a deceptively calm tone.

Ava dropped her eyes to the floor, her knees threatening to give out. She quivered noticeably.

"Don't make me—" Sir Waters began, but he was cut off by another student's voice.

"Sir, I can shift with her."

Ava's heartbeat accelerated, her glossy forehead covered in a sweaty sheen. She didn't dare look up to see her new savior.

"Gulati?" The professor pulled his chin back in confusion. "Well, all right then. Get on with it. Contrary to what you students seem to think, I do *not* have all day."

Ava's curiosity won out—again, a cat thing—and she hesitantly dragged her eyes from the fascinating floor to see who had been speaking. Right as she did so, the boy stepped directly in front of her. Her heart crashed into her mouth. It was him. The impossibly pretty boy from the ship. Tarun.

She swallowed. It should be a crime to look as good as he did. How does he get away with it? He had a face that could make any female melt with just a hint of a smile. Powerfully built, but tall enough that it didn't make him look too bulky. And his long, luscious lashes—really too long for a boy—starkly contrasting his shocking white hair, all suited him perfectly somehow. Especially when those strands of white hair kept falling into his eyes like that.

And he was staring right at her.

"Hey, remember me?"

Okay, he was talking to her. Actually talking to her. Even though everyone at the school knew what she was now. She needed to say something back... But... How did people form words again? Okay, wait, he was holding out his hand now, what was he trying to do? He didn't honestly believe she was going to reach out and shake it, did he? That would make her melt into a puddle at his feet. Nope. She would keep her hand right where it was, thank you very much.

"Not much of a talker, now, are you?"

Air whooshed from her head. This couldn't be happening.

"Okay, it was Ava, right?"

And he remembered her name...

"Don't worry, I'll get you through this. I used to practice this with my dad all the time." He sounded so calm and confident, his deep voice striking a chord inside her chest that made her heart pound faster.

She just nodded stupidly.

"Are you sure you're okay?" He studied her. "Can you say something?"

"Schlaflyserwster..." *Oh. My. God. Someone please kill me now.*

His eyes widened. "Alrighty then." His lips quirked, a tiny mute movement, but amusement lit up his eyes. His left cheek dimpled adorably. "Go on, I won't bite, I promise."

Ava let out a sound. Was that a giggle? Coming from her? She didn't think she had the ability to sound like such an airhead, but there it was.

What the heck was wrong with her? She was fine with him on the boat—well, sort of—and now she was acting like she'd taken too many blows to the head.

Taking a different approach, Tarun grabbed her hands and pulled her closer to him, both of them standing in the sun now. His eyes blazed at her through his lashes, a perfect mix of dark and light, just like everything else about him. As she stared, wishing she could stroke those cheekbones, or perhaps bite his—"Oh!"

"Oh!"

"Meow!" She hadn't realized it had happened, but she was now about ten inches long, perched up on her hind legs, digging her claws into his hands. *Curses*. She morphed into her tabby while fantasizing about this boy right in front of her.

Something similar had happened in the past while daydreaming about other things. She couldn't help it though—she was a daydreamer.

Tarun didn't miss a beat. Within seconds, Ava's tiny claws were digging into pads of soft, white fur. Tarun was a *tiger*—a *white* tiger! And he stood directly in front of her, gazing back at her with his also very catlike eyes. Never mind the fact he was over ten times her size, he was also a cat like her.

At that moment, it all started again. The laughter. She'd recognize that squeal anywhere. It was her devilish roommate, Elaine.

Ava had quickly come to realize whatever had possessed Elaine to help her out that first night was apparently a one-off situation. She had gone right back to being a horrible brat to Ava immediately after the opening dinner.

Tarun growled from deep in his throat and then paced back and forth. Ava had been so absorbed in herself and the surrounding laughter she hadn't taken a moment to appreciate the majestic beast before her. Like his human body, he was nothing short of magnificent. A mixture of dark and light. His coat shone brightly in the sunlight, so brightly it was almost blinding. Ava had to retreat several steps back just to see all the way up to his head. His luscious white fur mixing beautifully with his black stripes. He looked back at her and retracted his claws when he saw her staring.

She let out an accidental squeak.

More snickers from the other students.

Tarun growled again, but louder this time.

Ava meowed, her hackles rising. Sure, she was tiny. Yes, she was an ordinary house cat, but that gave him no right to growl at her as if she were his subordinate, dammit! She'd had it up to her neck with everyone mocking her, and now it was coming from him, too? She'd be damned if she was going to stand there and listen to it.

Almost automatically, as if she had no control over herself, she reared back and took a swipe across the white tiger's flawless face, leaving three streaks of blood across his pink nose.

He staggered backward and sat down on his haunches in shock.

With that, mind completely made up, Ava turned and sauntered from the room. Sir Waters's call for her return fell on deaf ears. Typical cat.

10

Waters looked on, trying to act unimpressed. Not once had either of the shifters spoken a single human word. Normally, he would be grumpy about that, because that was the bloody assignment after all, but he was sure there was some sort of communication going on between the cats, even if he couldn't understand.

The little cat and the tiger seemed to be an excellent match.

Interesting. He made a mental note to pair them up in the next year's competition. It made perfect sense that that little tabby-cat girl would have some tricks up her sleeve, especially considering who her father was. And their resemblance was uncanny. There was no mistaking her.

Tarun angled his head and watched Ava run off, his breath hitching to his throat when she crashed into the doorframe. It hadn't stopped her though. She just picked herself right back up and kept running. In the wake of her leaving, the rest of the class wore similar looks of befuddlement. Although everyone else had only seen her strut away with what looked like confidence. But he was the only one in the location where he could see her take off at a run when she thought she was out of everyone's view.

He wondered what possessed the other shifters to act the way they did. After all, none of them would appreciate being mocked for what they were born to be.

It was difficult for him to relate because they had always respected him for what he was, but having grown up around other shifters, he had definitely seen it get ugly between the predators and the prey. In fact, he'd had to step in on more than one occasion to defend his best friend, James, for shifting into the tiniest creature in their friend group back in England.

The alpha male in him yearned to go after her, to console her and wipe off the tears he was sure would be running down her face. But the tiger in him, proud as he was gentle, would have none of it. He knew she would be all right without him. At that thought, the bell rang, signaling the end of Sir Waters's class.

The students let out a collective breath. They had all survived their first class with the notorious English tortoise-knight.

Tarun moved away from the light and morphed back to human and into his jeans and black T-shirt, grateful they could easily shift in and out of their clothes here at the academy. Whatever magic the academy had allowed that to happen. Back home, when he shifted, if he didn't take off his clothes first, it ripped them to shreds, and then he would end up shifting back naked. That made for some awkward situations.

A couple of his "friends" approached him— Deacon and one of the bears whose name he couldn't remember. He'd noticed an alliance of predators forming. While the dragons, birds of prey, dolphins and sharks, wolves, and the original Aussies stuck together, a motley crew of assorted predators had formed as well: Deacon, who was a gorilla shifter he'd known back in England, a few bears, a puma, a rhino, and a pretty female polar bear. And they seemed adamant to get Tarun to hang out with them.

But Tarun was having none of it. From what he could tell, they were all jerks.

And he wasn't even surprised none of them made a move to go after the girl they'd all practically laughed out of the room. He was even disgusted with himself.

But then James cut in to his rambling thoughts. "Let's get some food, Mate. That always makes you feel better," James said to him, patting Tarun on the shoulder.

Tarun was so grateful to have James there at the school with him. He never would've imagined James would get in to Animage Academy with him —he was a hummingbird. But now, because of the new policy...

"Come on, Mate, what do you say?" James spoke with his thick English accent.

Just as Tarun was about to answer his friend, another voice cut him off.

"We totally should."

Elaine. Great.

The eagle shifter was walking with her other bird-of-prey friends and angled the group in Tarun's direction.

Tarun glared at her. He wasn't ready to talk to her—in fact, he wanted nothing to do with her, at least for the time being. Tarun clearly heard her distinctive jeering at Ava, even though—as he knew full well—she was her roommate.

"Did I miss something?" Elaine batted her eyelashes.

"We're just going to get food," James blurted out.

Tarun rolled his eyes and groaned.

Poor James was still clueless to the fact these stuck-up jerks were only talking to him because he was friends with the Great White Tiger.

The entire group moved toward the classroom door, pushing out as a solid unit. It opened into a brightly lit hallway. In the hall, they met up with the other two bear shifters—Tarun couldn't place their names either—and a couple more birds of prey.

Feeling ridiculous, he moved through the hallway and entered the cafeteria with this group of shifters. He quickly scanned the area, hoping Ava had at least come for food. He ignored the murmuring from several of the birds of prey, and even a few of the dragon girls, were making about him, and made a beeline for the food. James followed closely behind.

Tarun looked back. Deacon had now caught up with the others and so had Elaine.

Good.

Tarun chatted with James as they collected

food on their trays. There was quite an eclectic mix of meals to accommodate all the different types of shifters. For instance, Tarun's diet consisted of almost entirely meat, as rare as possible, but James was practically vegetarian.

"Hey! Tarun! Over here!" It was Jen, the pretty polar-bear shifter from Norway he'd met at the orientation dinner.

With a shrug, he made his way down to the end of the long table where she had reserved seats for him and—surprisingly—James. It wasn't long before Deacon and the other predators came to join them.

As Tarun settled in between Jen and James, he surveyed the room again. Most of the shifters were tearing into assorted meats, except for the aquatic shifters, they passed on the meat, opting for different types of seafood instead. The birds, which included James, picked at grains of rice mixed with a few legumes here and there.

The noise in the room was deafening. He had to shout every time he wanted to talk.

But scan the room all he did, he didn't see her.

He selected a chicken leg from his tray in one hand and a bratwurst in the other, dipped each of them in a cup of gravy, and mowed down.

"She's here."

Tarun dropped the bratwurst on his plate,

splattering gravy in all directions. "Ava?" Although because his mouth was full of meat, it came out sounding like "Effer?" but it didn't matter, because James wasn't listening anyway. Instead, he grunted impatiently. "It's *her*." He jerked his head toward the direction of the door.

Tarun's eyebrows disappeared into his hair. In all the years he'd known him, James consistently surprised him. He already had a crush on a girl here? His eyes followed James's gaze to make sure he was looking at the right girl.

When he finally settled on the fact that yes, they were looking at the same girl, Tarun had to admit James had taste. She was tall, curvy, and extremely beautiful. Smooth skin that was extremely dark. The color stood out beautifully against her light plaid uniform dress. Tarun guessed she had come from Africa, considering her full and smooth features.

She stood at the entranceway for several seconds before stepping into the room. Then she scanned the scene with her eyes before stalking over to a table. As she approached, the dolphins and the sharks pushed their seats closer together to prevent her from sitting with them. The birds of prey, Elaine and her flock, barely spared her a look, and definitely not a seat.

The majestic girl kept her chin up and didn't

react to the rudeness being directed at her from all sides. As she moved closer to where Tarun and James were sitting, Tarun could make out her shifter mark on her right arm.

"Oh wow, James, an elephant?" He didn't bother to keep the astonishment from his voice. "You definitely set your sights high, literally." He chuckled at his own stupid joke. "I've not actually ever met one before, not an African elephant, anyway. I met a few Indian elephant shifters back home in India when I was a kid, but they liked to keep to themselves. And they are usually rich as sin. No offense, Bro, but she might be out of your league."

But it didn't seem like James was listening. His eyes were glued to her. Tarun realized he couldn't stop James from what he was about to do even if he tried. His friend's pale blue eyes lit right up the minute she entered the cafeteria, and he hadn't stopped bouncing in his seat since.

Tarun figured he might as well try to help his friend out, at least. After all, the other shifters seemed to reject her, although Tarun couldn't imagine why. Didn't they know how powerful she was? How powerful her family must be? Was it possible no one at the school realized the status of elephant shifters? They should fall all over themselves around her.

"Why don't you ask her to sit with us?" he finally said. He had to; James looked like he was close to sliding off his chair to the ground. And Tarun was certain that, in a few seconds, he'd probably start drooling. And that would just be downright embarrassing for both of them. Plus, that was not an image he wanted in his head.

"Are you sure? You don't mind?"

"What are you talking about? Invite her over." Tarun laughed when James jumped out of his seat, nearly toppling it over in his haste. His belt loop caught on a chair at one point, and Tarun laughed even harder, watching his friend scramble around as he made his way over to the girl.

Tarun couldn't hear what James was saying to her, but he must've said something witty because she was bending over forward in laughter. After a few more seconds, James led her over to their table, his crooked teeth flashing in the light, walking with a swagger Tarun had never seen before.

"Hey, Deacon, can you move down? Just one seat?" Tarun asked, lightly prodding Deacon in the side.

Deacon looked up, disgust apparent on his face. "Why do I have to move for the elephant?"

That was it, Tarun thought. Deacon was possibly the biggest jerk at the school. Any sliver of hope Tarun had been holding on to about maintaining a friendship with him was destroyed right then and there.

He gritted his teeth. "Just move, Deacon, you don't want to get on my bad side today," he growled, sounding angrier than he meant to.

Deacon glared daggers at him before shifting his backpack and scooting his food down the table, moving not one but two seats down.

That's right, you ass, Tarun did not say.

James, who was too busy doting over his love interest to notice the minor spat between Deacon and Tarun, nodded approvingly and pulled out Deacon's freshly vacated chair for her.

Tarun, meet Winta. Winta, this is my best friend, Tarun," James introduced them.

"Hi, Winta, it's really nice to meet you," Tarun greeted her, shaking the hand she extended. It was soft and plump, like the rest of her.

"Thank you. You as well," she answered in her deep but feminine voice. Her accent so heavy it came out sounding more like "Tank yo."

James put a hand under his chin as he smiled at her and said to Tarun—even though he was still looking at Winta—"Don't you just love the way she talks?"

Oh my God, James. Tarun slapped his forehead with his palm. "We all have accents here, James, especially to the Aussies. Remember the first time you said that to me when we were kids and I told you it was rude?"

"Oh—oh—oh—" James stuttered. "I'm so sorry, Winta! I didn't mean to—"

"It's fine." Winta smiled at him with her bright white teeth. "I like the way your accent sounds, too."

James turned beet red.

Tarun chuckled at the situation. Winta seemed really cool, and perhaps she even liked James. He could only hope for his friend's sake. He thought back to when he had first met James. They were both eleven. Tarun had just moved to England from India with his parents.

James lived in the flat next door, and they met when James had spotted Tarun's shoes on the front porch and knocked on his door to let him know. Together, at that young age, they had a good laugh about the different customs in Eastern countries versus Western countries. That was how Tarun learned he wasn't supposed to leave his shoes outside in England.

"So where are you from, Winta?" Tarun tried to change the direction of the awkward conversation.

She tapped her long fingers nervously on the table, all traces of laughter suddenly gone.

Unfortunately, James grinned continuously as

he heaped food unceremoniously into his mouth, then, even more unfortunately—with a mouth full of food—he offered her some from his plate.

⁻She raised an offended-looking eyebrow at him, but he still didn't notice.

In a small voice, she answered, "I am from Kenya." Her 'r' in 'from' particularly long and pronounced.

"Where in Kenya?" Tarun had actually been there a couple times with his family, so he hoped maybe he could connect with her on that because she seemed suddenly nervous.

Her eyes flashed briefly before she swept her curly lashes down again. "I doubt you'd know where." She grabbed the cutlery, apparently deciding James wouldn't poison her, and stabbed a cherry tomato off his plate.

"That's okay, you can tell me later." James's grin was getting creepy. He hadn't even bothered to sweep his straw-colored hair away from his forehead—a habit Tarun had become accustomed to seeing.

"Mmmhmmm," Winta mumbled, then shut her eyes and hummed in appreciation. "That tastes *sooo* good. Do you think they grow these fresh in the garden?" she drawled, referring to the cherry tomato.

James's elbow slipped off the table, nearly

knocking down his glass of water. Tarun cringed, but he couldn't blame the guy. Winta was like an Egyptian goddess, especially right at that moment with her neck thrown back like that, eyes closed, and the expensive jewelry glinting off her ears and neck.

Yeah, Tarun completely understood, but James was getting worse by the second. At some point, Winta may have turned to ask the simple question, but James panicked and knocked his plate to the ground. It landed with a resounding clatter. Everyone suddenly went quiet, staring at him.

Tarun thought James was beet red before, but that was nothing compared to how furiously he blushed all the way up to the roots of his hair now. He ducked beneath the table to try to clear his mess, missing the comical expression Winta tossed at Tarun before ducking down after him.

"And I thought *I* was the awkward one," Winta joked, scooping bits and pieces of rice back onto the tray.

Tarun smiled brightly as he leaned under the table to help them. It seemed like perhaps James had found a perfect match.

Although the tension defused with Winta's teasing, by the end of the lunch hour, James had made little recovery.

Finally, the bell rang, Winta surged from her

seat like it was on fire and hurried out the double doors.

James stood, as if to go after her, but he caught Tarun's eyes. Tarun made a gun with his fingers and pretended to shoot himself in the mouth.

Deacon and the others laughed heartily. And even Tarun couldn't hold back his smile.

James looked up at the ceiling and took a deep breath. "I need a real gun to do just that," he said with a groan and stalked out of the cafeteria.

11

The day dawned bright and clear. No hint of a cloud in the sky. Birds chirped cheerfully on the oak tree, which happened to be close to her dormitory window. A cool breeze wafted from the quiet ocean to the room. Ava dragged her comforter over her head and groaned.

It was another perfect day.

Stupid perfect days.

Her godforsaken roommate was also up already. Ava could hear Elaine humming from the bathroom, even with the shower running. It was only a matter of time before the entire flock flooded into their room. A morning ritual that took place almost every day. They waited for the queen to dress, helping with her hair, picking out her clothes, selecting shoes—

even manicures and pedicures were frequently part of the procedure—all the while twittering and chirping about the boys. Or mostly just the one boy.

Tarun.

Some days, he was all they talked about. He's so cute. He's so funny. His accent is so sexy.

So far, Ava had learned all about him without even having to take a step from her bed. The color of his eyes—that topic was dissected for almost twenty minutes and cut short only because they had to leave for training. But one also can't forget about the way he walks, his voice, his hair, ugh!

And the squeals. Oh, the squeals. Or squawks, definitely squawks would be a better term. Damn bird girls. Ava really hoped she didn't sound as much like a pathetic little kitten as Elaine and her friends did like squawking birds.

One time, they had all screamed so excitedly, with their high-pitched bird calls, that Ava had bolted from the bed and hit the floor in her alarm, ready to run for her life for fear there was some disaster.

For the first time in her sixteen years, Ava genuinely wanted to say damn all consequences and murder them one by one. It would be fitting; a cat ripping out the throats of birds. When the ringing in her ears finally reduced, she'd discovered Elaine had apparently scored a kiss from Tarun.

Lovely.

They would make such a stunningly attractive couple.

But today—today the chaos hadn't started yet. Although she tried to bury herself under her pillow, she knew she couldn't hide forever. It was already getting hot and suffocating under the heavy comforter as the sunlight filled her room. But she cherished these quiet moments every morning, so she delayed for another several minutes before finally throwing the comforter back and allowing her feet to touch the floor.

If only she could force herself to wake up significantly earlier. She slid her feet into her flip-flops and crossed to the window. If she were a morning person, she could have hours of quiet time instead of minutes.

Looking out the window, she gazed at the Sacred Tree, forever fascinated with it. So many leaves. She wondered about the story behind each and every one of those shifters. She thought about Priya, and imagined the fun the little girl would have coming up with those stories.

Beyond the tree, she could see a few students already out and about.

Next, she padded over to her dresser, the one on her side of the room—the side *not* covered in puke pink. She then removed the plaid dress she was required to wear on school days, and a pair of black heeled boots. She'd given up on her Converse for the time being. Choosing to fit in better instead. Although she wouldn't have admitted to anyone out loud that was why.

She tossed the dress on the bed, hanger and all, and stepped out of her pajamas. Just as she did so, Elaine's humming stopped.

Ava steadied herself for Elaine's reappearance from the bathroom.

"You know what would just be so nice?"

Ava didn't even turn to look at her. "What might that be, Elaine?"

"To enter this room without perceiving this reeking stench."

Ava rolled her eyes. Sometimes, when Elaine spoke, especially to her, she tried extra hard to sound smart. But sentences like that, little did she know, made her sound like a snotty moron. The *reeking stench*, as she so eloquently called it, was Ava's lavender body mist. A completely natural conglomeration Lucy made for Ava before she left for the academy. She enjoyed the smell, and it reminded her of home. And it was nothing compared to the Chanel perfume Elaine practically bathed in every morning. Frequently, Ava would still be coughing by third period from having to inhale so much of it. And she swore she could even taste it in her food.

Ava bit her tongue, resisting the urge to indulge Elaine's bullying.

With no response from Ava, Elaine prattled on. "It's absurd, you know. And to think, you're from Miami!? I thought people in Miami had class and taste..."

Ava didn't hear the rest because she had already retreated to the bathroom and closed the door behind her. She quickly turned the shower on to drown out Elaine's shrill voice. *Whatever, like Pasadena is really so much better,* Ava thought, which was where Elaine was from.

After her shower, when she returned to the room, Elaine's flock was already there. The incessant chattering filling the space.

Five of them. The one bouncing on Elaine's bed was Lorraine, the hawk shifter. Just like Elaine, she was blonde with blue eyes and big boobs. Breanna, standing next to Elaine in front of the mirror, her red curls bouncing as she put makeup on, was a falcon shifter. Diane and Daniella were twin raven shifters, each with pale skin and long dark hair—very Edgar Allan Poe but sexier. And then Lois, the platinum-blonde owl shifter, reclined on the fluffy pink rug, browsing through a fashion magazine.

None of the girls spared Ava a single glance. Fine by her. She shrugged into her uniform, only partially listening to them. Drowning them out completely was impossible when they were in the same room. Then, as she headed over to her vanity mirror to brush out her long brown hair, she picked up on part of the conversation.

"...was talking to her, I swear it."

Ava paused mid stroke and turned, not knowing which one of them had spoken. They all sounded the same to her, aside from Elaine, who she could tell apart because her voice was the highest in pitch.

"What? That clumsy thing?" Lois prattled.

Were they seriously talking about her while she was right there? That was low, even for them.

"Yeah, I saw them talking under the oak." That was Daniella.

Okay, maybe they weren't talking about her.

"She's so gross though." Ava watched Lorraine through her mirror. She was talking nonchalantly, as if talking smack behind people's backs was a perfectly acceptable activity.

"Nooo!" Elaine screeched. "Who does that?"

"Apparently he has no taste or class—ouch! Diane, watch the curling iron!" Breanna wailed.

"Sorry!" Diane slackened the cord and moved slightly to the left. She was curling the ends of Elaine's hair for her. How precious.

"Well, why do you think Tarun hangs out with him so much then?" Elaine looked at herself in the mirror as if questioning her own reflection.

Breanna just shrugged.

"What's her name, anyway?" Lorraine asked, dabbing another coating of red lip gloss onto her already overly glossed lips.

"Winter... Wanda... Juanita... Something," Lois suggested.

They all giggled.

"Are you sure it's not Shaniqua, or Laquinta, or something?" Elaine said, an evil smirk on her lips.

At that, all the bird girls cackled even harder.

Ava froze, accidentally dropping the hairbrush right into her lap. She knew exactly who they were talking about now... She had to stomp one foot on top of the other to keep herself from losing her cool too quickly.

She swung around to confront them.

"Her name is Winta!" she shrieked. They all

paused and stared at her. Elaine just scowled, but Ava didn't care. She plunged right on. "Her name is Winta, and James is lucky she gives him the time of day! She's way out of his league!"

"Pretty sure you got that backwards, Tabby," Breanna mocked her.

"James may be a tiny little bird," Elaine cut in, "but he hangs out with the other predators, so he's definitely out of her league." She folded her arms haughtily.

Ava flushed, and not prettily, then jumped out of her chair, the hairbrush falling out of her lap to her feet. "Yeah? You mean like Tarun is out of *your* league?"

The girls gasped collectively. It was a low blow, and Ava knew it, but she was past caring. Besides, they started it. They all knew full well Winta was Ava's best friend at the school. Which meant they started talking about it with her in earshot completely on purpose.

Elaine stomped toward Ava, although she tottered dangerously on her heels before she steadied herself. "You will regret that, *Roomie.*" Her voice was deceptively calm, as was the smile playing on her hot-pink lips.

"Oh, I'm so scared." Ava shivered dramatically.

Daniella coughed discreetly behind her palm. None of the other girls dared interrupt the charged silence. Elaine's evil smile disappeared, and she stared down at Ava, unblinking. "You should be," she deadpanned.

Ava smirked back at her, doing her best to come across way more confident about this than she felt. "Oh, it's on." Then she picked up her backpack, threw it over her shoulder theatrically, and strode out of the room.

Once Ava made it outside, she met up with Winta who'd been skulking in the shade of one of the gum trees.

Apparently not noticing Ava's distress, Winta just locked arms with her and went on about their usual best-friend chatter. "I mean, I had to talk to that guy! You took so long! He approached me under the tree, and I couldn't get away because I had to wait for you where I promised I would. But you were late!"

Ava blinked. "You mean James? I thought you liked him."

"Yeah, he's cute and all. And he seems nice— when he's not making a complete clown out of himself—but what am I going to do with a hummingbird? I'm an elephant! Everyone will laugh at us. Every. One."

Winta's behavior surprised Ava. She slowed down and turned to look her friend in the eyes. "Winta, that's not something you should worry about. And honestly, I'm surprised you even are. If you like him, then you gotta go for it."

"How can I know if I like him if I don't even know him? It doesn't sound worth it. Not to be the laughingstock of the school for the next four years." She pushed her tongue into her upper lip. She did that whenever she wanted to make a point clear. It was as if to say, 'I dare you to argue with me.'

But Ava wasn't having it. "So what if they laugh? That's practically all they do at this stupid school. And if they're going to do it anyway, it certainly shouldn't prevent you from living your life."

Winta pulled her arm away from Ava's, and crossed it over her chest with her own. "Yes, oh Mighty Sage One. How ironic of *you* to say that."

Ava looked away for a moment. "What?"

Winta silently assessed her friend, hiding her smile behind her long, elegant, and manicured fingers.

Ava wondered briefly where Winta had received that manicure, but she shook it off. Winta had plenty of artistic talents. She probably did it herself.

"Something is going on with you," Winta accused. "I can tell by the ticking vein in the side of your temple, right there." Winta reached one of her sparkling fingernails up and tapped the side of Ava's face.

Ava batted her hand away.

"I had a rough morning with Elaine is all. And her flock. They are so awful." She wiped a few strands of hair away from her face. In the weeks she had already spent at the academy, she still had yet to get used to the constant draft from the ocean. Although, she recently learned the ocean was not as she thought. Even the sky was a glamour. The school really was several miles underground. Growing up calling it the shifter school down under was apparently completely literal.

"Watch it, Trumpeter."

Ava looked around. It was Kiki, another random Aussie. A wombat, if Ava remembered correctly. She opened her mouth to ask what that was about, but closed it again immediately. *Trumpeter. Like an elephant's trumpet. Got it.*

Poor Winta, she was now as disliked as Ava. Ava couldn't help but feel a little guilty. She wondered if perhaps Winta wouldn't be getting this so bad if she didn't hang out with her.

She could still hear Kiki giggling as she joined

up with a few others, and Ava lost it. "No, you watch it, you stuck-up twat waffle!"

Winta jumped back, clearly alarmed.

Kiki just stuck her tongue out and flipped her the bird. *Very mature.* But at least that was it. She and her friends kept walking.

"Ava, really, what crawled up your butt this morning? You deal with Elaine and her flock every day. What made this one affect you so much?"

The two friends were entering the reception area now, specifically, the same reception room where she had to reveal herself the first day of school, right through those double doors. She still thought about that horrible moment every time she walked through them.

Inside, shifters were heading in all different directions. There were hallways and training rooms on all sides, and the colossal granite counter straight ahead, where Headmistress Levine stood, serenely watching her students move around.

Prior to coming to Australia, Ava had never seen let alone spoken to a griffin shifter. They were one of the rarest animals known. Probably, the only shifter more rare than a griffin would be a unicorn. But unicorns were completely extinct now. Or supposedly... Ava still wondered about that unicorn dust. But Headmistress Levine was a powerful griffin shifter, even though Ava had never seen her transform. Nor had anyone else in the school that she knew of. It was rumored that when she did so, Headmistress Levine stood over twenty feet tall with a wingspan that stretched from one end of the great hall to the other. That probably explained why the headmistress preferred to say in her human form.

Headmistress Levine nodded slightly toward Ava and Winta, acknowledging them like she did every single shifter as they passed her. Her squinting eyes kept contact with Ava's for a little longer than was comfortable.

Shaking off that creepiness, Ava finally answered. "Elaine was in rare form," she bit out. Spitting the name out like it was poison.

"What could she possibly have done this time that would be worse than any other time?" Winta questioned her. "You can't keep letting her get to you when you know this is how she is."

Ava glowered at her friend. "It's not funny. That girl is Satan incarnate, I'm telling you."

Winta's eyes widened, genuinely terrified. "Don't mention his name out loud like that!" she warned.

Ava looked at her, confused, then remembered that where Winta was from, her family believes, firmly, maybe too firmly, in the devil's potency. Having not grown up religious, it was difficult for

Ava to relate to, but she knew Winta was dead frightened of the consequences.

Before it could progress, Ava simply waved her hand, cutting her off. "Sorry. But she's so impossible. Nothing I do is right. If I talk wrong, if I move wrong, if my perfume is wrong—"

"But your perfume is wonderful!" Winta leaned in and sniffed Ava like a dog.

Ava laughed loudly and playfully pushed her friend away. "I know, right?"

Winta laughed, too.

"Seriously, I have to wake up every morning to a squawking feathery eagle knocking things all around the room, and she can't handle a little tabby cat? A tabby! She complains I get cat hair on everything, but that's a lie, because I rarely morph anywhere in the room other than my own bed when I'm asleep, and I would never ever touch her stuff... But does she listen? Nooooo."

"She's despicable," Winta quipped, but the corner of her mouth turned up.

Ava smiled back at her, grateful Winta was no longer asking questions because she certainly didn't want to tell her what Elaine and her friends had actually been talking about that morning.

It looked like Winta had been about to say something else but quickly snapped her mouth shut, knowing she needed to stay quiet as they passed the training rooms already filled with students waiting for teachers.

The classes were divided up differently in different situations. The land animals could all learn together on certain days, whereas the water animals took to the "ocean."

Other days, the classes were divided by seniority. The first-years were together and the fourth years—or the seniors—were off in combat training.

Through the window at the end of the hall, in the distance, Ava could clearly make out sharks, jellyfish, seahorses, octopuses, whales, and even seals getting ready for their lessons. Just as she was wondering where the dolphins were, a group of them rushed past them, almost knocking Ava's purse off her shoulder as they squeaked and chattered. Probably all late for class. The dolphins reminded her of the cheerleaders in her former high school, whereas the sharks reminded her of the jocks—or specifically just the football players. And just as football players tended to date cheerleaders, so the sharks and the dolphins paired off. Oddly enough, Ava had only seen two female sharks and zero male dolphins.

Grateful she didn't have to train in the ocean— she hated water, another cat thing—she looked away from the dolphin girls disappearing out the glass doorway at the end of the hall.

The land animals trained in rooms tailored to their sizes and features. Which was why, today, she had to leave Winta for two whole classes.

"I'll see you at lunch?" The girls stood together at the door to Winta's upcoming class, target practice. Behind Winta, through the door of the classroom, Ava could see moose, giraffes, elk, gorillas, bears, dragons, and a rhinoceros prancing around. She would die before admitting it, but she was fiercely grateful to the school for creating the system. Otherwise she'd worry constantly about getting trampled.

"Sure, of course. Oh, and Ava?" Winta turned and faced her friend. "Don't let her get to you, seriously."

Ava just nodded sheepishly, realizing she'd been complaining about Elaine all the way to class. Feeling foolish, she spun around—not an easy feat on her stupid pointy boots—and set out for her own class, bracing herself for Elaine and whatever horrors her training held for her.

12

Her training room held about fifty shifters already. Although Ava had an uncanny ability to recognize and remember someone's face, even if she only saw them once, names still escaped her. When she was young, twice she'd forgotten the name of her own pet—what ever happened to that poor guinea pig?

She wrapped her fingers around the ornate door handle and pulled back, sucking in air, her lips set in a straight line, and closed the door behind her, turning to face the next hour of her day.

She still couldn't believe the training rooms sometimes. It didn't even feel like school. Of course, she was previously used to a normal high school class, filled with desks and chairs and what-not. This was just so different.

Firstly, this room was circular, no corners. Along the walls, cushioned seats faced the podium where the instructor stood to teach. There was a board behind there, which was a little more typical but rarely used because most of the classes were practical. But occasionally the teacher sketched out certain moves for them or tried to write notes and key points when they were explaining something.

And, to be fair, it made sense that they wanted the students to learn theory and practical demonstration. Besides, the headmistress insisted. On the other side of the wall, behind a protective glass case, were stored materials of all sorts. Some of them were bizarre, like saddles, muzzles, whips, and maces. There were a few assorted blades, and even sets of nunchucks and rope darts. Ava hadn't seen any of these items in use though, and she wasn't in a hurry to change that.

As of now, all the shifters needed for training was to learn better coordination and fine-tuning.

Well, in her case, she needed a little more than that.

She took her place toward the back. There were five rows of ten seats, and she took the last on the right. Although most of those seats would be pushed back when they began the hands-on training. She pulled her hair forward to cover most of her face and her shifter mark as best she could as she unpacked her books and her notepad and pens.

She was looking through the notes she took in her previous class when a noise at the entrance distracted her. Too late, she looked up and caught his eyes. In the midst of the noise, and other boys slapping his back and shoulders, practically salivating for his attention, Tarun stared back at her.

For a moment, Ava felt like he'd caught her in a web. She tried to break away, but she was lost staring back into those bewitching catlike eyes. Not even realizing she was doing it, as she was used to hiding lately, she tucked her hair behind her ears, exposing her smooth aquiline neck.

Tarun's breath wedged in his dry throat.

Good God, she was flawless. How is it she didn't have every boy in school fawning all over her? Or even the girls at that?

As the class filled up, he could only see the top of her head from where she was hiding in the back, but that was enough. But when someone moved away, bringing her fully into his view, she revealed to him another layer of her exquisite beauty. That long beautiful neck.

He shook his head. *Okay, it's just a neck.* He needed to get a hold of himself.

He was shaking from his reverie when Colin called out to him from his chair, interrupting his thoughts. Colin was a vulture shifter and normally hung out with the birds of prey. But Tarun thought a rat would have suited him better—or maybe a weasel. He had known Colin from his time living in England, for they also lived near each other, and Colin used to torment James relentlessly when they were growing up.

All the seats were filling up fast as students claimed them. And everyone sitting in the seats facing the entrance had straightened their spines and looked ahead with attentive eyes. Tarun knew that meant Professor Bills had arrived.

Seeing as how there were now no other choices, he scurried over to sit next to Colin. He had been keeping up somewhat of a charade with these other "friends." Not exactly telling them he didn't want to be around them, or that he didn't really like them at all, but keeping it amicable as best as possible. Even though he didn't want them as friends, he certainly didn't want them as enemies either.

As he settled in, he snuck another glance over

at the pretty kitty. It pained him that Ava didn't seem to like him very much. But he supposed he couldn't entirely blame her because she probably concluded he was like all the other jerks that laughed at her. He did hang out with several of them, after all.

And even though he hated the stupid segregation of the school, the segregation everyone tried to pretend didn't exist, he knew if he started associating with her, it would probably only cause her more problems at this point.

As Professor Bills started speaking, Tarun poured all his energy into preventing his wayward neck from whipping back to stare at her. Instead, he ripped open his bag and got ready for training.

"This won't do at all!" Professor Bills, a balding, rotund owl-shifter, bellowed from the podium. Tarun had missed whatever he just said, being so focused on the contents of his bag. Apparently, Colin and his other friends had, too, because they all went mute.

A small white hand flitted to Tarun's forearm. His eyes followed it all the way to the face of its owner, and he met with Elaine's bright blue eyes.

He hadn't even seen her sitting behind him. She was everywhere! How did she do that? He smiled uncomfortably at her and patted her hand.

Was that a sigh? Did she just sigh? No, he

must've heard wrong. Why did he just touch her back? That was clearly a terrible idea. It was bad enough he'd kissed her hand the other day, and that was only because she'd shoved it in his face. It would have been rude not to. She acted like such a princess all the time, but the worst part was right after he did, she ran off squealing to her friends about how he'd kissed her!

"Everyone, step out from your places, please!" Professor Bills bellowed again. It was unnecessary for him to be so loud because everyone in the class could hear him just fine, even if he spoke in his normal voice. He was just that loud of a man.

As Tarun moved to his feet, he made eye contact with James several seats over. James looked nervous. Tarun briefly wondered why, seeing as how Winta wasn't anywhere nearby, but his thoughts were interrupted by Bills's booming voice once again.

"Everyone in a circle! Around the room!" Bills demanded.

One by one, the entire class lined up, their backs toward the wall as they faced Bills in the center.

The professor was wearing a velvety blue suit that did nothing to hide the wide expanse of his jiggling belly.

Tarun had heard one of the younger students,

Priya, he believed her name was, make a joke that that belly swallowed all the students who refused to listen.

After an unnecessarily prolonged silence, which Bills spent walking from one trainee to the next, sniffing the air in their faces like a dog trying to remember a scent, he stopped in front of a short girl with long black hair.

Tarun turned his head slightly to see the person Bills had chosen as his first victim. Her face had blanched. She was definitely small for her age, which Tarun assumed was sixteen because she was there with them, and she didn't look at all comfortable. She looked as if the faintest of winds could blow her away. Her uniform dress hung almost to her knees, probably because that was the smallest size the school had, but even then, she was practically swimming in it.

She stared fixedly at her shoes, quivering noticeably, awaiting her instructions.

"I want to show you the power behind your abilities," Bills bent down and said directly into her face, "and who better to reveal it than—" he turned and opened his arms dramatically as he said to the rest of the class, "a phoenix!"

Everyone gasped, including Tarun. He had no idea there was a phoenix shifter at the school. How had he not known about her? Next to unicorns, and right alongside griffins, the mythical phoenix was as rare as could be and nearly extinct. There were only a few known left in existence.

As the astonishment sank in, the stunned silence turned into gasps of wonder, words of amazement, and a few students near her even boldly reached out to touch her.

She whimpered and folded in on herself, all the while keeping her gaze locked firmly on her fascinating Mary Jane's.

"Miss Sharifi," Bills asked in the softest voice Tarun had heard the booming man use, bending down his sizable hulk to her height with much difficulty. "Can you show us?" His voice wheezed a little at the end.

"Yes, Sir."

Tarun could barely hear her little voice.

Even though he thought he had braced himself for it, nothing could have prepared Tarun for what happened next. He'd read the legends about these creatures, heard the stories, but discarded most of them as false. But now, raw proof stared back at him in the form of this tiny girl.

She stepped away from the line, toward the center of the circle, directly into the light streaming in from the long windows. It was cataclysmic. First, little licks of flames erupted from every part of her body. She spread her arms wide and slowly turned in a circle for all to see.

Tarun gulped and waited for Bills to tell her enough was enough, but the professor looked on, his eyes glued to the spectacle in front of him like every other shifter in the room.

The suffocating smell of burning skin filled Tarun's nostrils. His eyes watered. Some of the others looked away uncomfortably, but no one attempted to get Bills to stop her.

So they all watched the tiny girl, the smallest he'd seen in their year, burn alive.

It was gruesome. The flames extended around her in the shape of an enormous bird, her arms deteriorating as her skin peeled off, and orange wings took shape around her. Her bones disintegrated, soiling the floor with the ashes, her hair shriveling up, eyes squeezed tightly shut until they burst inside her sockets, leaving a dark emptiness behind. He'd seen many shifters transform, but never had he seen something as gruesome as this. The only thing that prevented him from running forward and trying to stop this was the fact that she remained perfectly calm. In fact, she wasn't even shaky anymore.

It was hard to believe this was the shy girl from just a few moments earlier. And even though the entire scene was terrifying and disturbing, she wasn't screaming in pain, and Bills stood confidently by her side, occasionally nodding his approval or patting his monstrous belly. Yes, satisfaction oozed from him in droves. He looked at the girl like she was his pride and joy.

"Magnificent, isn't she?" he called out to the classroom. Then, directed toward the flaming bird shape in front of him, "There is no fear in your power, no shame, no restraint, only acceptance!"

When the last shreds of her body crackled and fell to the floor, the fire burned brighter, licking hungrily at the air. Enveloping. Encompassing. Tarun couldn't see any part of her body any longer. Only vicious flames.

Professor Bills brought his palms together and waved them back and forth in satisfaction. "When you do this, once you fully accept it, you have access to your powers, both animal and human."

Tarun had no idea what that meant, but the words were scarcely out of the professor's mouth when the fire winked out completely, as suddenly as it appeared. In its place were the powdery ashes of the girl who'd stood there just before.

Okay, now things were getting a little unnerving. What was Professor Bills really trying to prove here? That girl had just burned up! Had he fully expected her to commit suicide while they all watched? And everyone stood by and let it happen?

His heart pounded as he processed the scenario. He knew phoenixes were known to resurrect from their ashes, but that girl couldn't have been older than sixteen, and the professor had made her kill herself! That was it. Her life snuffed out. So now she would come back and be reborn? And have to start life all over again for the teacher's sideshow entertainment?

"Sir? I don't understand. What just happened?"

Out of the corner of his eye, Tarun saw Ava peeking out behind her curtain of brown hair. She didn't seem overly flustered. Good for her. He felt ready to tackle that fat man.

Her question was the icebreaker, because after that, the entire class broke into mini pandemonium. Everyone broke the circle and started backing away from the pile of ashes. One question climbing over the other.

"That's a brilliant question, Miss Carrington," Professor Bills responded without looking at her. Then he turned to Tarun. "Mr. Gulati, are you familiar with the legends of the phoenix?"

Preparing to speak over all the noise, Tarun's shoulders jerked up and down. "I am, but I guess that's all they are: legends. I don't have any confirmation of their—" Tarun broke off, stunned, as he stared at the ashes.

They were glowing, and not just the cinders, but the whole pile was actually glowing. Then they lifted up and started to swirl. Every particle moving and multiplying until they started to come back together. Bonding, attaching to each other.

Tarun rubbed his eyes, literally, to make sure he wasn't dreaming. Smoke suffused and inundated from the powder, whining and squealing, twirling around, faster and faster. Next, thick clouds of cinder and embers rose, all-consuming, soft and fiery at once.

It was taking the shape of... Really? It was forming into a human. Then a huge plume of powdery smoke exploded all around the shape, and when it collapsed and settled, in place of the human-shaped ashes, stood a bright red, yellow, and orange regal phoenix.

She was alive! Tarun was astonished, sure, he went to school with dragons, and his headmistress was a griffin, and heck, even he was a walking legend—a white tiger. Yet that knowledge did nothing to defeat the wonder of what he had just witnessed. He had no idea watching one shift would be so...magical.

"Bravo, Miss Sharifi, bravo!" Bills called out, beaming. The regal creature spread her wings—

her squawk could be heard, likely all the way down the hall and perhaps even outside. It even drowned out the vigorous clapping of all her classmates as she then took off into the air proudly—thankfully, the ceiling was several stories high in that training room for this very reason—and zipped down close to the students in line so they could feel the heat coming from her. Then she careened off toward the ceiling again.

"Now, each of you will do exactly the same." He ignored the looks of surprise from his students. "You will harness the power endowed to you as human and animal!"

Murmurs of confusion filled the room.

"Miss Anderson!"

Michaela stepped out from her place in line, perhaps wondering if the teachers had had some sort of secret meeting to decide on making her into a spectacle in every single class. Tarun had certainly wondered that about her himself.

"What are pandas known for?"

She let out a little giggle before replying, "Food!"

Professor Bills glared at her, pushing his mouth all the way to the side of his face.

"I mean, um, strength?" she ventured, looking as if she expected Bills to discipline her again.

But he said, "Good. What are cheetahs known for?"

Her eyes shot from side to side, but her face remained angled at the professor. "Speed."

"And wolves?"

"Agility..." She trailed off in a whisper and then went on. "And tracking."

"Yes, good. And you will demonstrate that now as a human."

Michaela's shoulders slumped as she groaned.

Tarun chuckled to himself. This was one of those things that made this academy so great. Every tiny little detail about any shifter could be picked apart and then harnessed into something the shifter could use in combat.

And that Michaela girl was about to be the first to figure it out...in front of everybody.

13

When it was her turn, Ava hesitated longer than was appropriate.

"Miss Carrington, I'm sure there is something house cats do that you can emulate." Bills watched her fidget nervously.

When she'd signed up for this godforsaken school, for whatever reason she'd been so excited about, no one had told her she would have to transform in almost every class. What was the use of consistently making her feel small and pathetic? She had just watched a freaking phoenix burn to death and explode from the ashes, for crying out loud! Couldn't that have been enough for the day?

Okay, think... What are tabby cats known for? Her brain went blank. She reached the recesses of her memory desperately. Searching for something cats were known for other than being lazy and sassy, and playing with balls of yarn. Anything cool. Anything even remotely not *uncool!* But she came up empty.

While she fidgeted, shifting her weight back and forth between her pointy boots, the sound of snickering filtered its way to her.

Great, here we go again.

Soon, Professor Bills would lose patience with her and come for her head, she was certain.

Okay, okay, something... Anything...

Inhaling deeply, she thought of something. Sure, it wasn't stunning, but at least she had something to show that wouldn't make her look like a complete and total loser.

"Sharp claws," she said finally, facing her instructor. Behind him, she could see Tarun. Relief printed clearly across his features. Weird. Stupid Tarun. Who did he think he was? Being nice to her one second and ignoring her the next?

"Go on then," Bills pushed when she just stood there.

Concentrating only on her fingernails, she isolated her shift to that area only, something she'd gotten moderately good at during her classes at Animage. She looked down and watched them lengthen into tiny-but-sharp glistening claws.

Bills squinted, his practically nonexistent eyebrows lifting slightly. "Curious," he murmured.

She returned his gaze with a questioning look.

Saying nothing, Bills hurried over to his desk, opened the drawer, grabbed a large hand mirror, and returned to where Ava stood, her claws still extended.

"Did you not mean to do that?" he asked her as he held the mirror up in front of her.

Ava looked at her reflection and didn't see what he was referring to at first, but then she noticed her eyes had changed as well. Her eyes were usually catlike anyway, but now they were one hundred percent her cat eyes. Her pupils reduced to small vertical slits. She let her tongue snake out, Yep, that too. She hadn't been trying to do it, hadn't even been aware of it actually, but now that she looked around, she realized she could see with her cat vision.

"That's a very helpful skill to have, Miss Carrington, you realize that?"

Night vision could certainly be useful, yes.

Nodding, Ava swished her claws through the air, let out a small hissing noise, and then without backing up for momentum, she leaped straight off the floor, high and tall, flipping in a full somersault when she got about ten feet up and then struck back down, landing comfortably on both feet.

Amazingly enough, she didn't even totter on her heels. Hooray for cat balance. Feeling a boost of confidence, she made herself twist again, but accidentally slashed her own arm with her razor-sharp claws.

Blood, thick and unrelenting, seeped from the wound, eliciting gasps of horror from those closest to her. Ava's heart thudded sporadically, her vision swimming. She hated the sight of her own blood. And now that she looked at it, the pain was kicking in—and that cut went *deep*. She bit down hard on her lip and looked at the ceiling to avoid letting herself cry.

Professor Bills didn't look too concerned and made his way over to his desk once again, setting the hand mirror down and replacing it with a roll of gauze. But, before he'd even made his way back halfway across the room, Ava noticed the pain was rapidly dissipating. She risked a glance back down at her wound, expecting to see sliced-open gore, but instead saw a purple glowing light coming from her arm and realized her skin had already begun to heal. The opening had latched back together, and it was no longer bleeding. There was still blood all over her arm, but there was no longer a blood flow. Just the dried mess from a few moments ago.

"Professor, Sir, she's healing!" Someone—she didn't know who—called from nearby her.

"Impossible!" Bills snapped as he waddled toward Ava, gauze in hand.

"No, she really is," the same person said again, this time a little quieter.

The professor scrunched his brows as he approached her and dropped the gauze as he grabbed her arm and pulled it toward him. "Well, I'll be damned." He moved so close to her arm that Ava could feel his breath on her skin. "I've only known one person who could do that. As far as I know, only one species of shifter has that ability."

Again, Ava didn't bother to control her curiosity. "Who?" she probed. She was even more shocked than the rest of the class, she was sure. Here she is, harnessing her animal power in her human form for the first time, and this is what she gets.

"Purple glow... Carrington... Of course." Bills was still staring at her arm. Was he talking to her or himself?

"Yes, that's my name. Ava Carrington." She was still befuddled.

He turned her arm over again and again. Checked over, checked under—perfectly healed. "Not even a faint scar," he muttered to himself. "Just like Matthew."

"Okay, and who is Matthew?" This was getting frustrating. Sure, she was always curious about things, but he was just being downright evasive.

Finally, Bills looked up from her arm and stared into her eyes. "I should've made the connection when I saw your eyes. Carrington. Matthew Carrington. You look just like him."

Without thinking, Ava snatched her blood-stained arm back, feeling her face drain of all color. She took a wavering step back, no longer feeling steady in her boots.

Maybe she'd heard him wrong.

No, that couldn't be. He was loud as a freight train, and he didn't mince words. So that just means... "You knew my father?"

His eyes widened. "Okay, everyone, that will be all for today," he announced hastily, clapping his hands a few times and waddling as fast as he could to the door.

The students broke back into their little groups, chattering and wondering what had just been discovered. Ava was left behind, clutching her stained arm.

Elaine had already found her way back to Tarun. But Ava turned away, not wanting to watch.

She briefly wished Winta were there with her at this moment, but she knew her friend was in her own training room with the other larger shifters, and they wouldn't see each other until lunch because they had no classes together until then.

Despondent, Ava turned her attention back to Professor Bills, or at least where she assumed he was still standing, only to find that he'd also left the room.

She looked around, confused, trying to figure out if she was supposed to wait for him or not. After a few moments, she finally made her way back to her backpack behind one of the seats pushed up against the wall.

Tarun looked back over his shoulder as he exited the training room to see if Ava was okay and what the professor was saying to her. But, of course, Elaine swept her way into his line of vision. Thankfully, James was standing next to him and asked Elaine a question—he didn't hear what— and that distracted her for a moment.

He paused at the doorway and found Ava standing in the back of the room, sorting through her backpack. Now there was no sign of Professor Bills. That was odd. So that meant the professor hadn't wanted to talk to her after class then? So she was free at the moment...

He turned to tell James he would see him later,

but, to his pleasant surprise, James and Elaine were now halfway down the hallway together. *Thank you, James.*

Gulping down a mouthful of air, he made his way toward Ava. He'd been so proud of her, watching her flounce with such power. Her partial transformation had been impressive, and he had even made mental notes to himself to try several of her moves himself. Side by side, in their human forms, utilizing those abilities, they would probably be fairly equally matched in a fight. And then he had felt his heart stop beating when that blood gushed from her. She went from looking so fierce to so fragile in just a moment. He was finding it difficult to put it out of his mind.

And then there was the matter of her healing... What had that been about?

Whatever had happened between Ava and the professor, he wanted to know.

She finished zipping up her bag, stood up from her crouching position, and threw it over her shoulder. Ava had already taken two steps forward before she looked up and noticed him standing there. She stopped and stared at him, saying nothing.

"Hi." Yeah, maybe not his best opening line.

She still didn't respond.

"Ava?"

Slowly, her expression changed from surprise to pain. He struggled to control the barrage of emotions that slammed through him when he saw that. Without invitation, he reached out and touched her arm—the wounded one.

She didn't back away from him; she just continued to stare.

"I know, you don't really know me," he blurted out. There, he was off to such a brilliant start. "And I probably have no business talking to you right now, but I just wanted you to know you can talk to me. About anything." Oh my God, why did he sound like such a loser? He normally had so much confidence. Especially with girls.

Contrary to what he was expecting—not that he really knew what he was expecting—she frowned at him. No, scratch that; she looked spitting mad, actually. "That's it? You're just here to scrounge for information? Why? Just so you can tell your asshole friends all about the tabby cat's problems?"

Tarun reared back, her words hitting him harder than a kick in the gut. "Fine. Don't tell me anything." Oh no, that came out way harsher than he intended. He softened his gaze. "Just know you have a friend if you want one." Then he turned to leave.

Ava sorely regretted her stupid outburst toward the handsome boy. She was normally more level-headed than this. But now that the words were out of her mouth, she couldn't exactly take them back. She wanted to reach out and apologize, but her pride kept her from opening her mouth. Instead, she just watched him walk away.

He took a few steps, then stiffened, and for a moment Ava thought he was about to say something else. But then his entire stance deflated, and he continued walking.

"Wait, Tarun, I'm sorry about that." The words just flew out of her mouth before she realized what she was doing. "I guess I'm just a little strung up about things right now."

He stopped and turned, not looking at all upset. He was even smiling slightly. Then the laughter tinkled out. "A little?"

Ava couldn't help but chuckle. "Okay, maybe a lot. But Professor Bills just reminded me of someone I'd rather forget."

He flashed his teeth at her in a kind smile. His eyes twinkling compellingly. "We don't have to talk about it. I just thought you might want to."

She relaxed her shoulders and flipped her hair backward. Trying to look and sound nonchalant, she said, "It's really no big deal. He mentioned my father."

His confusion was obvious. Ringing her slender fingers, she continued, "My father, well... He left...you see, when—no—*before* I was born."

He remained quiet, but continued to stare at her with his steady gold-flecked eyes urging her to go on.

"You know, my time here at the academy is probably the most I've talked about my dad. I'm not even sure if he's still alive. But then today, out of the blue, Bills straight-up says his name to me like it's nothing."

Tarun simply nodded and whispered, "Uh, wow."

She got a little more animated. "Not a letter, not a word, *nothing* from him for my entire life! We just pretended he didn't exist. And sometimes I feel so stupid because I still want to know him, and I want to know why he left us like that..." She allowed herself to trail off as she realized she was telling way too much of her personal story to a practical stranger. What had possessed her to tell him all that?

The only person here who really knew anything was Winta, and even she only knew bits and pieces.

"Hey, Ava, it's okay, and I don't think you're

crazy or stupid." He squeezed her bicep a little as he spoke. How had she not noticed when he put his hand there? Now she was more than aware of his touch.

"I think, if I were in your situation, I would want to know him, too." But then he shrugged. "Although I'm not in your situation, so I can only speculate. Sorry."

"Where are your parents now?" She angled her head back to look at his eyes.

"They're in England." He lowered his hand away from her arm. She now felt its absence.

"They moved me there from India when I was eleven."

"I see." She tapped her bottom lip with her finger. "So that's how you know James then. And Deacon and Colin and the others?"

"Yeah, as I mentioned on the boat, there were a lot of shifters in that area. And a lot of them are still there now, because they didn't come to the academy."

"And both your parents were tigers, too, I assume?"

Tarun nodded. "Yes, and they are both white tigers. Very unusual that they were both the only white tigers of their litter. So of course, their marriage was arranged to produce me. And I'm the only child they were able to have, so they want the best for me, but they also keep me on a short leash."

"I suppose I can understand that." She was beginning to feel more relaxed about him. He seemed more authentic as she got to know him.

He leaned in closer to her and lowered his voice, even though there was no one else in the training room with them anymore. "Don't you ever get curious about him? Your father, I mean?"

"Of course!" she answered quickly. "I literally just told you that."

He smiled sheepishly, obviously feeling a little stupid for what he just said. "I mean, now that you're here, aren't you curious to find out more? Because I'm sure we can find a picture of him."

Ava didn't answer right away. It was finally dawning on her that her father had probably attended the school. She should have realized that the very second Professor Bills used his name. And now that she thought about it, it made something Sir Waters had said on the first day of class make more sense as well: "Ava Carrington, we finally meet." She had forgotten about that. "My father was a student here." She whispered the statement. It wasn't even a question anymore.

"I'm sure he must have been," Tarun agreed. "And I can help you find him."

On the other side of the door to the training room, Elaine shifted her weight uncomfortably in her Barbie heels. Utilizing her bird hearing, she could eavesdrop on the entire conversation.

That stupid little kitty, with her wide gullible eyes, painting herself to Tarun like an innocent victim. But Elaine knew there was something deeper, dirtier, about her idiotic roommate.

She just had to find out what.

Elaine snuck a peek at them, and then she rolled her eyes at the sight. The nerve of that stupid cat! Seriously? She thought she could get that close to Tarun? As if she even deserved to breathe the same air as him. Oh, she was going to show her.

Whoever her father was, he certainly couldn't have been anyone important. And Elaine was going to see to it that Ava's embarrassing secret about her deadbeat father got out.

14

Lunchtime came, but Ava skipped it.

Out here in the courtyard she felt a little more at home. The fresh air drifting in from the ocean, the scintillating, enchanting scents coming from the plants. Hundreds of them —lilies, roses, chrysanthemums, irises...everywhere she looked there was a new flower to see. Bursting with colors, most clustered and climbed over the brick walls, lined the walkways. She plucked three white roses, red ones, too.

"So no one told you life was gonna be this waaayyyy..." she sang the *Friends* theme song, sticking the roses in the sides of her hair.

"Your job's a joke, you're broke, your love life's DOAaaa...." she sang again, smiling, already feeling the calm that came from watching her favorite show back home, take over. At first, when her mother binge-watched it, Ava wanted to hurl the TV at the nearest wall; then one day, there was nothing to do but watch it.

So, she pressed play and became addicted to their simple lives. She loved Chandler the most; he was funny and sarcastic. Rachel was a spoiled brat, and Monica a clean freak. She spent hours arguing with her mother about Ross and Rachel. On a break? Not on a break?

Personally, she believed they were on a break, Ross was heartbroken that night and Chloe was available.

Her favorite show wasn't enough to distract her from the fact she was hiding behind the Sacred Tree, peeking out at the sharks, birds and other predators. Like Ava, they had come out to play in the fresh air.

Watching them frolic in the water and fly off in the air filled her with untold sadness. Ava was fine on her own, but sometimes she wished she could be like them—wished she was bigger, like the dragon shifters, sharks, kangaroos, and the graceful, playful dolphins.

Now, even from her position behind the tree, she could hear Elaine and her flock laughing with the bigger cats. Of course Tarun was there, too. She told herself all she felt for Tarun was purely platonic and left it at that. He was just friendly.

Where was Winta anyway? They were supposed to meet here.... Ava reached for her uniform pocket to check her cell phone. Then she remembered she didn't have her cell phone. Even after more than a month without it, she still unconsciously reached for it. She had no idea what time it was, but she could only guess Winta was at least fifteen minutes late.

Looking across the walkway, she forced her eyes away from Elaine's simpering adoration of Tarun. Good Lord, her roommate was truly insufferable.

She then made a concerted effort to keep her attention on two sharks splashing through the water, shifting back to human as they leaped through the air and then returning to shark form as they splashed into the water. They must be third- or fourth-years because that was a pretty cool trick. It definitely took some skilled shifting.

She was pretty sure they were dating. And yes, she knew that was the type of relationship pretty much all the students preferred. And not even just the students, but most shifters worldwide. Shifters frowned upon mixing species.

Keep it simple. Avoid complications. Same species, same country, same groups of friends. She couldn't blame them, not really. Watching the two sharks swim around each other made her realize how easy it was. She'd heard that old saying many times: "A bird may love a fish, but where would they live?" Ava wondered if the person who said that originally was actually a shifter. She closed her eyes for a moment and envisioned one of the dolphins in love with one of the birds of prey. Sure, those particular cliques got along well enough, but she never heard of them dating each other. And they usually went at each other's throats hard-core in the competitions, from what she'd heard.

But, said a voice in the back of her head, *you and Tarun actually makes sense. You're both in the cat family.*

Ava shook the thought away.

Then she thought about Winta and her attraction to James. It was a fair point. How would that relationship ever work? Would he move back to Africa with her to live with the other elephants? African shifters were known to be big and powerful, after all, as most of them were very impressive animals. Elephants, lions, tigers, leopards, gorillas. Sure, there was a baboon, or meerkat here and there, but one never heard much about them. Or would James try to bring his beautiful girlfriend, who was a solid five inches taller than him anyway, back to England with him to meet his humming-bird family?

Ava smiled sadly at the thought.

Anyway, it was nothing to worry over. It didn't matter. Winta had decided not to pursue James, and Ava knew, sure as hell, she wouldn't end up with Tarun.

"I found it," Winta called out excitedly.

Ava turned as her friend came to stand beside her.

Winta had released her curls today, and they bounced around her face as she jumped from one foot to the other, practically bubbling with the news of what she discovered.

"What? So fast?" Ava was genuinely surprised. It was only the previous evening she had told Winta about what Professor Bills had said about her father. She certainly hadn't expected news so soon.

"Yeah, of course. I am Researcher Extraordinaire!" Winta took a little bow. "Come on, I'll show you. It wasn't easy though, so I'm pretty sure you owe me lunch now." She shot her friend a sassy wink.

Ava chuckled, linking her arm through Winta's. "Sure do. Just add it to my tab."

They turned and headed back toward the school. Ava didn't see or hear him sneak up, but she jumped and let out a startled hiss when Tarun landed behind her and grabbed her shoulders.

She glared at him, fully aware she had hissed at him like a cat and that her hair was a little puffier at the moment because she raised her hackles.

Tarun just chuckled at her. "You weren't going somewhere without me, right?"

"Tarun! You scared the bejeezus out of me!" Ava wailed, although her smile said otherwise. And curse those silly grins she was finding it harder and harder to suppress every time he got near her.

His smile was unrepentant, "Am I that scary?" Then he looked over his shoulder. "James, am I that scary?"

James, who was currently picking flowers from the bushes, looked up so suddenly he stumbled into the bush. "Hmmm? What did you say?" Then he detached himself from the bush and trundled over to them.

Winta couldn't take the wait much longer and yanked on Ava's arm. "You told him? Before me? Seriously?" she asked, dragging Ava along. The boys followed behind.

"He was there when it happened! Not my fault!" Ava defended. "And he suggested this, by the way."

They were at the double-door entrance when

Ava looked back to see if Tarun and James followed. They had, but she also saw Elaine. *Ugh.*

Elaine had started to follow Tarun, jabbering away, as usual, but then stopped talking mid-sentence, her mouth open and hand in the air, when she saw where he was going...and with whom. Her chest rose and fell noticeably, and she narrowed her eyes—her hot-pink lips in a thin line. Ava didn't have to speculate much to know Elaine was furious that Tarun was having anything to do with the tabby cat.

Great. Another reason for Elaine to hate her. Not that it mattered at this point. Although Ava's lips turned up slightly at the satisfaction of knowing Elaine was actually jealous of her budding friendship with Tarun. *Serves you right,* Ava thought.

Her concerns about Elaine and her petty problems dissolved from her mind the moment she and Winta stepped into the school's extremely ancient library.

Because she had been opting to get outside as much as possible since she made it to the school, rather than be cooped up, this was her first time inside the library itself. And it was quite a sight to behold. Like every other part of the academy, it was overwhelming—in size and ornate decoration. Massive shelves, mounted side by side, stretched from one end to the other, top to bottom. Set up like dominoes. That would be quite the mess if one domino fell over! There had to be hundreds of thousands of books. Ava couldn't even see the end of one shelf. And every single one was stuffed full.

Students, mostly foxes, wolves, rabbits and a few assorted others, sat at wooden desks, crouched over heavy dusty tomes. Someone dimmed the lighting to an uncomfortable level, even in the reading areas. And it smelled like dust, leather, and burned wood. Ava didn't care for that scent though, it gave her a headache. Honestly, she didn't like being inside at all. Back in Miami, she'd been part of the track team, which meant a lot of time outside, just the way she liked it. And during the summers, she went to the beach with her friends. Her mother always said it was weird that she was so outdoorsy because house cats were supposed to prefer the indoors. Lucy certainly did.

Winta seemed to know exactly where she was going. Weaving between the shelves, carefully avoiding ladders, she finally stopped in front of a shelf marked "Alumni."

Ava stepped right next to her. "So many year-books," she breathed. The shelf alone was huge. It went from floor to ceiling, so these yearbooks probably went back several hundred years.

The four of them, Ava, Winta, Tarun, and

James, stood together looking at the plethora of books in awe. "Our names will be in here soon, too," Tarun whispered.

"Indeed." Winta nodded.

"Have you ever been down here?" Tarun asked James.

James twiddled the flowers he plucked from the bushes between his fingers. Ava assumed he just hadn't gotten the nerve to give them to Winta yet. "Sure, once. What are we doing here?" He watched Winta as she traced her finger across the spines of several books in a row.

"Matthew Carrington, Ava's father, supposedly attended Animage," Tarun explained.

"Oh, really?" James's eyes grew wide. "So he must have been way more than a tabby cat then, right?"

"Dude." Tarun glared at him. "Way more than a tabby cat? What the hell is wrong with you? Do you hear yourself when you speak?"

Ava just shook her head. Winta ignored all of them.

"No! I just mean that, being a tabby-cat shifter wouldn't have gotten him into this school. Unless maybe he was Australian?"

"I guess that's possible," Ava agreed. She hadn't thought of that, actually. But that could really be the only explanation. The academy never would've allowed a non-Australian tabby-cat shifter.

"There's no way." Tarun scrunched up his brow. "I mean no offense, Ava, but even as a native Australian, Animage wouldn't have allowed a tabby-cat shifter before this year. There are a lot of Australian wolves that didn't even get in unless they came from a rich and powerful pack. This school has always been super selective."

"Until now," Ava grumbled. "And still, none of us know why."

"Hey now, I'm not complaining," James pointed out. "I wouldn't be here either if it weren't for the new rule. So I get it, Ava."

That was true. Of the four of them standing there, James was definitely the only other one who really understood. But he knew exactly where his parents were. So it still wasn't quite the same.

"But you seriously didn't know your dad used to be a student here?" James asked Ava.

Ava shook her head, her hair falling in front of her face as she did so. "No idea. My mom never talked about him. And I don't even know if he's alive. I've never met him. I couldn't even get her to tell me his name until a few years ago."

"I'm so sorry." James looked at his feet. "Here." He shoved the flower at Ava.

Ava looked down at the flower in surprise and

then cast a sideways glance at Winta. Winta was looking at her with an expression of...well, Ava didn't know what that expression was. Confusion? Amusement? Jealousy? She really had no clue. "Oh. Well, thank you, James." She accepted the flower from him, not knowing what else to do.

James grinned, but then looked at Winta, and his face fell, clearly thinking he had made a horrible mistake. He opened his mouth, as if to make some sort of excuse, when Winta put him out of his misery—she cleared her throat loudly. "Got it!" She pulled one yearbook from the shelf and started thumbing through it.

"Is that really it?" Ava questioned her. "How do you know?"

"Well, if it isn't this one, it will be one of these." Winta tapped her pointer finger on the adjacent yearbooks to where the one she was holding sat on the shelf just moments before. "He would have attended between ages sixteen and twenty. You think he was around your mother's age, which you said is forty, so if he was born forty years ago, he would have attended the academy between twenty and twenty-four years ago, so..." Winta extended the yearbook she was holding out toward Ava and gave it a little shake. "This should be right in the middle of that timeframe."

"All right. I can't argue with that logic. Very well done." Ava gave her friend an approving nod.

After a few moments of silence, Winta slammed the yearbook shut. "Okay, it's not this one," she said as she grabbed hold of the ladder in front of her, stepped up one rung, and slid the book back in among the others, extracting the one next to it in its place.

Same thing.

This time, Winta pulled down four yearbooks and handed one to each of them as she stepped down to the floor.

Each of them opened to the front few pages and started scanning the table of contents.

After looking through the names, at the bottom of the very first page, Ava saw it: Matthew Carrington. "I found him," she whispered. "I found my dad."

The others looked up and closed the books they were holding, giving her their full attention. They gathered around her. Winta put a comforting hand on her shoulder, and Tarun slid his hand against her lower back. Normally, Ava would freak out about that, but she was too busy freaking out about this now instead.

She closed the yearbook again and admired the black leather front cover. There was a stamp across the front with the griffin seal, just like on her application.

Ava's heart went into overdrive. The implications were limitless. Perhaps she could finally know who the man was that abandoned them. She would finally get to see what he looked like. Maybe she could even track him down, if he's still alive, and punch him in the face for leaving, and of course get an apology for her mother. "I'm so nervous." She wiped her palm on her dress and then petted the griffin seal on the cover.

"I'd be nervous, too," Winta agreed with her. "It's a big deal."

Ava smiled tightly. She was too strung up to walk over to the desk chairs. So instead, she just plopped right down on the tiled floor, crossed her legs, and opened the book again. Her friends piled down next to her, leaning in close.

She turned to the first page.

"Oh, is that Levine? She looks the same!" Tarun exclaimed.

Ava nodded absentmindedly, flipping the pages quickly, even sneezed hard at the dust a few times. Apparently no one thought to clean these books...ever.

She saw Professor Bills and Sir Waters as well. Neither of them had aged as gracefully as Headmistress Levine. Shockingly, Professor Bills used to be quite handsome.

"The page numbers are so faded it's hard to even read them!" Ava complained. Several minutes of page flipping—and a bit of cussing—later, she stopped. "That's him."

"Oh, wow, it sure is!" Tarun agreed. "You really do look just like him!"

Ava sat there staring, open mouthed, at the picture of a boy, dour faced and serious. "My mother is blonde," she whispered, running her fingers over it. His hair was brown, that ugly, dirty brown, just like hers. And his eyes, his eyes were just like hers as well. She wondered what kind of cat shifter he was. Why was there no mention of the students' shifter species in there along with their name and graduation year? Shouldn't that be important to mention? And also, why hadn't she taken after him—whatever he was—instead of her mom's tabby? Interestingly enough, his eyes didn't look quite as catlike as Ava's, but they were definitely the same eyes.

His roughly cut hair was down almost to his neck, and he had an impish, slightly mischievous look about him. His nose turned up at the end, very much like Ava's, and his upturned collar proved he didn't much care about his appearance.

"Yeah, Ava, if you were a boy, that's what you would look like, for sure," James agreed.

Ava tried to chuckle, but it suddenly clogged in her throat. "But why didn't mom tell me?" she asked, more to herself than the others.

"She must have had a good reason," Winta offered, petting Ava's back.

But that wasn't what Ava wanted to hear. Without being able to control herself, she spat out, "Damn her stupid reasons! I deserved to know!" She shoved the book off her lap and jumped up in one leap.

"Ava," Tarun cooed, trying to put his arm around her, "it's okay, just calm—"

Winta tried to wave Tarun down as he attempted to soothe her, but it was too late.

"Don't tell me to calm down! This is all their fault! Both of them! Every day, I feel lost. I don't know anything about that half of me. I didn't even know my hair was dark because of him!"

She started to pace back and forth down the aisle. "First thing I'm gonna do tomorrow morning is write her a very scathing letter. She is going to get quite the earful—or eyeful, I guess... Whatever."

"Yes, you could do that. *Oooor*, you could find out more..." Tarun suggested.

"But the letter first."

"Are you always this impulsive?"

"Shut up, Tarun."

She was in no mood to be talked out of her very justified anger. Her parents had betrayed her. Both of them. And she would make them pay. Both of them. Assuming her father was still alive, anyway. She would find him, and she would make him sorry.

15

"Please, and I will not ask you again, get out of my way," Tarun growled. He stood in the hall just outside the library, facing Elaine, Deacon, Colin, and a few of their friends.

Just what he wanted. It turned out Elaine had followed him and watched him go into the library with the others, and then gathered reinforcements. Was she even capable of *not* causing drama?

Almost every passerby couldn't resist staring as he raised his voice at the pissy bird.

Ava and Winta had already walked off, for obvious reasons. And he couldn't blame them for not wanting to deal with Elaine. But James still stood by his side, the faithful and consistent friend he was.

"Don't tell me you've fallen for her little innocent act because that's all it is, you know: an act," Elaine insisted.

"I didn't fall for anyone, Elaine. You gotta stop this crap. What exactly do you even want from me? Do you just not want me to have friends, or do you want me all to yourself? Is that it?"

"No! I mean, you know what? You can have as many friends as you want. But I would think you would know better than to hang out with *her*." Her voice dripped loathing.

"She's right though, you know," Deacon added in. "I mean, I get it. I think she's hot, too. But not at all worth talking to. And her little woe-is-me act is pretty sad. She obviously just wants attention."

"There is no woe-is-me act, Deacon, don't be such a jerk." Tarun knew there wasn't much of a point in arguing, but he couldn't help wanting to defend her.

"You should really be more conscientious of who you spend your time with," one of Elaine's flock—Lois he thought her name was—spoke up this time. "Present company does not suit you." As she said the last words, Lois gave James a side glance.

James stiffened next to him.

Oh, no, she did not.

"None of my friends have done a single thing to

you." Tarun said the first part to Lois, and then he turned his attention back to Elaine. "They've done nothing to deserve the way you treat them, which is like dirt."

"But that's what they are if you think about it. They're filthy little animals. Well, except for the massive one—she's a filthy, gigantic mass of a beast."

Tarun knew exactly what was coming, and he threw his arm out to the side just in time. James had tried to leap forward to attack Elaine for what she said about Winta. Tarun couldn't blame James, but he knew that would not help the situation. None of the school staff would welcome James attacking Elaine. They would probably suspend or even expel him. Especially because Elaine had a prestigious family, and James was just a hummingbird.

"Elaine, listen to yourself. Do the words you're spewing honestly make sense to you? Ava is the sweetest, kindest person I've met in a long time. She's honest and friendly. Something you wouldn't understand." The further on he went, the more flushed his face felt. His palms folded in on themselves, tightening into fists. Sure, he had restrained James, but for now, the only way he prevented himself from pouncing on that bitchy bird was by reminding himself that he was taught never to hit a woman. He could feel his tiger just itching to come out and take care of her.

Her jaws snapped and popped intermittently from the gum she was chewing as she stared back at him, stroking her long blonde hair. Considering her vacant expression, he wasn't sure she'd even heard what he'd said.

"Everything okay here?" One of the library attendants had heard the commotion and come out to check.

Tarun took a few steps backward and jerked his head up and down. "Everything is perfect, Mr. Jerome."

Elaine also nodded her head in agreement and then had the audacity to reach over and interlace her fingers in Tarun's. She twirled her hair between her slender fingers, rolled her eyes, and stretched a plastic smile across her face.

As the library attendant grunted and walked away, Tarun yanked his hand away from Elaine so quickly it felt like he could have pulled something out of socket. Fortunately, he hadn't allowed himself to give in to his urge to hurt any of them, after all, there was a zero-tolerance policy at the school for fighting—pretty important rule when you have a school full of people who turn into wild animals. He stalked away. And he'd missed it, but James had already gone.

Elaine, with a flip of her hair, gathered Lois and her other stupid birds, and started after him, but—thankfully—maintained her distance. He could still hear them squawking. Deacon and Colin must be close as well because Tarun could hear their voices in the mix.

But he did wonder where James had gotten off to...that conversation couldn't have been fun for him to witness.

The next class was as awkward as could be because they were all together. It was a class for predators only, so James, Ava, and Winta weren't there. But Tarun was stuck with Deacon, Colin, Elaine, and the rest of her ditzy flock.

He had taken the shortcut from the library to his next class just so he could avoid any more confrontation than necessary. It was general training in the largest training room in the school. The same one the oversized shifters used for combat training on Mondays and Wednesdays. He would have skipped the class that day, but it was Headmistress Levine's class, and missing it would have been, well, bloody.

So he did his best not to interact with the others as much as possible. He went through the motions, morphed when he had to, roared, pretended to stalk his prey, and roared some more.

He usually liked Levine's class. It allowed him to indulge the tiger within him. She taught them how to hunt as the animals they were. Which is why it was strictly for predators. There wasn't much she could have trained a hummingbird to do. And after all, it was imperative for them to learn how to survive in the wild as well as indoors.

And of course, at one point, the headmistress had teamed him up with Elaine. He was hoping to avoid her the most, but, to his relief, she studiously avoided him as well. She even avoided his eyes when they were forced to attack each other. She gave a half-hearted attempt at dive-bombing him and dodged out of the way just as he made to swipe at her with his massive claws. A few more times she got close enough to be touched, but she flounced out of reach before he could get to her.

Fine by him.

By the end of class, he was more than ready to go. Entering the hallway, he immediately caught a whiff of Ava's scent as she waltzed past him. Her head held high and shoulders straight. Winta at her side.

"Elaine's right, you know," Deacon said, appearing at Tarun's side and noticing the direction of his hungry gaze.

Tarun rolled his eyes. "About what? Don't tell me she's gotten to you, too?"

Deacon adjusted his backpack on his shoulder. "I'm just saying she's right. Ava is a little tabby cat. Everybody here makes fun of her. And *you* are the legendary white Bengal tiger. People look up to you, Tarun."

"What the hell are you trying to say?" he questioned him as they turned to Gold, their dormitory.

"Just that you are one of the best shifters in our class. You have a lot of natural talent—heck, maybe you're the best shifter in the entire school. You might be better off if you stayed away from her. And you know I'm not the only one who thinks so," Deacon finished, stopping at the entrance to their room.

Tarun desperately wished James had been assigned as his roommate instead of Deacon. Then he wouldn't have to listen to this.

Deacon leaned on the wall next to the door, facing the stairs. That way he could greet people and be social while he still talked with Tarun.

"I'm pretty sure I'm allowed to feel however I like about whoever I please," Tarun huffed. "I've never heard any of you complain about James, and he's a smaller animal than Ava!"

"Are you kidding me?" Deacon raised a disbelieving eyebrow. "None of us would put up with James if you didn't insist on keeping him around all the time." He shifted his shoulder away from the wall and leaned in toward Tarun. "You'd be better off without him, too. And I think you'll figure that out as your time goes on here. When you leave the academy in four years and join the shifter combat district, like you know you're destined for, it's not going to help you to have a hummingbird buzzing around your ears. You might as well get rid of your dirty laundry now."

Tarun clenched his fists so tightly at his sides he couldn't even feel his hands anymore. But hey, at least he hadn't punched Deacon in the face yet. So that was good. He was about to raise his voice, but stopped himself, took a deep breath, and then said calmly, "Believe it or not, you can't tell me who I can or cannot talk to. I'm so over this. Just go back to your nasty little narrow-minded world and maybe bring Elaine with you." He kept his tone calm and deadly. Tarun knew he sounded like his father whenever something had really upset him. He pushed past Deacon to walk into the room, but Deacon pushed him out of the way, darted into their room, and slammed the door in his face instead, locking it behind him.

"Oh, and tell the others, too," Tarun hollered through the closed door. Then he remembered he was still in the hallway, and people were staring. He looked up, smiled tightly, and headed back toward the stairwell. Apparently he was going for a walk instead of returning to his room right now. It was probably going to be very awkward between him and his roommate for the next few days.

16

Back in her room that night, Ava yanked her comforter over her head and unfolded the page she'd stolen from the yearbook. Oh yes, Mr. Jerome, the library attendant, would have a conniption if he found out what she did to school property. Illuminated by her flashlight, she stared at it all over again. Since the moment she left the library, thoughts of her father had consumed her.

There was nothing in that expression of his to suggest why he'd become the type of person to abandon his family. Sure, he looked serious, but who does that? There had to be so much more to this story. There had to—

Her blanket was suddenly yanked back, and Ava looked up to stare into Elaine's pinched scowl.

Ava just groaned inwardly. It was way too late at night for Elaine's drama. What did she even want now?

"This is all your fault!" Accusation dripped from Elaine's tightly strung body.

Ava sat up, only half amused when she noticed Elaine had big black tear streaks running down her face. "You're gonna have to be more specific." She pushed her comforter all the way down and swung her feet off the bed.

Elaine, for once, did not look perfect. Her hair was all over the place, mascara smeared down her cheeks, and even her clothes looked extra wrinkled. And were her socks mismatched?

The eagle whipped her right hand so close to Ava's face that it almost made contact. Ava reared back. "What the hell are you doing? You almost hit me!" She shifted farther back again before Elaine actually slapped her. The bird was obviously unhinged.

"He was mine, and you ruined it," Elaine hissed in her face.

Ava had to wipe the spray of spit off her forehead. *Okay...disgusting.* "Wait, is this about Tarun?"

"Damn right it is. Do you really think you can take him? Like that will actually work. For how long?"

"I didn't take anything or anyone. And he's not

up for the taking. He's his own shifter with his own mind. He makes his own choices. If he chooses to spend time with me, that's not your problem." Ava felt no guilt. Why would she back down from something like this? She had done nothing wrong.

"Whatever act you're putting on might be working right now, but he will eventually see through it," Elaine kept going. "And when you take what's mine, I will take what's yours."

What the hell was that supposed to mean? "Yours? What are you even talking about? Last time I checked, you and Tarun weren't dating, despite the fact you keep throwing yourself at him, so I don't see the problem. He doesn't even seem to like you very much."

"What did you just say to me?" Elaine lurched back, stomping her feet. A few feathers shot out of her pajamas. Oh boy, she was pissed all right.

"Way to act like the school tramp, Ava," she sneered.

Ava stood and stepped closer to Elaine calmly. "We both know who the school tramp really is. And it's definitely not me," Ava returned.

Elaine squared her shoulders and narrowed her eyes. "Whatever. I've been watching you." She sniffled, still trying to sound tough.

Ava stood up a little straighter, feeling more

confident as she went on. "Of course you have. I'm adorable."

Elaine ignored her jibe. "I know your type. You're just a sad little wannabe. A tiny little kitten who wants to be a great big wildcat. But you're not. And you may think you can take him away, but he's going to figure out what a poser you are soon enough. But I can see right through you, and I'm already so sick of you!"

Ava took a deep breath. She realized Elaine was all squawk and no bite right now. Clearly, she didn't know how to process her own emotions, so she was taking it out on Ava, the closest person in her vicinity. "If you want him so badly, why don't you just tell him?"

Elaine was noticeably taken aback. Clearly she'd been expecting a fight, and Ava had simply knocked the wind out of her sales with a few words. But Ava knew better—she wouldn't give her a fight. That wouldn't go well for her.

"Well, maybe I will," she mumbled. "And then you can cry under your covers when he chooses me. But I see what you're doing. You're just trying to get under my skin, and it won't work."

Ava pinched the bridge of her nose. "Look, Elaine, do whatever you want. I don't care. I've got a headache coming on, and frankly, I don't give a rat's ass if you marry Tarun tomorrow. I just want to go back to bed."

Elaine's hands flew to her hips. "There you go again!"

"Ugggghhh. Nothing shuts you up! I can't make you happy, even when I said you can take him and I don't care. Just stop your squawking and leave me alone!" Ava started to turn away from her.

"Don't you dare talk to me like that!" Elaine's face was pinched to the point of ridiculousness. "And don't you turn away from me! I'm not done yet!"

"Oh my goddddd, Elaine. Really? Ever since I got here, it's just been one problem after another with you. You don't let me rest, you don't ever shut up, and you aren't even nice to me. If you want to get rid of me so badly, just tell Levine I scream in my sleep or something and get a different roommate!"

"I tried to get rid of you from the first day, but they don't allow roommate changeovers!" Elaine stomped her feet again.

So there it was. That made sense. Elaine would've gotten rid of her if she could have. Weirdly enough, that stung. But Ava refused to let Elaine's rejection get to her. "Well, if that's really what you want, I'm sure you are clever enough to come up with some excuse to get rid of me. Lie if you have to." She crawled back under her covers and then looked back up at Elaine. "And as for Tarun, I don't really know what's going on there between the two of you, but maybe if you stopped acting like a raging bitch all the time, he might look at you twice. Good night." And with that, she threw herself down on her pillow theatrically and pulled the comforter over her head once more.

17

Three days after the cataclysmic fight with Elaine, Ava packed all her clothes and removed the sheets from her bed for the very last time in that room. Elaine and her flock talked loudly about her from the other side of the room as if she weren't there, making her feel even worse about the situation.

Elaine had made up some horrible lie about Ava having serious bowel problems that made her impossible to live with because of the stench. Reluctantly, Ava had played along because she wanted to get out of that room almost as badly as Elaine wanted her out. So, even though it was humiliating, Ava had pretended to burst into tears in front of Headmistress Levine, tearfully admitting that sometimes she just couldn't control herself. What a great way to start the week.

She had requested to move in with Winta, but Winta was still sleeping outside, and Michaela already shared the room where Winta kept her stuff. But apparently Levine was able to find her another "perfect fit." It turned out there was a student in their year over in Indigo Dorm that had virtually no sense of smell—strange because she was some kind of dog-shifter. Levine figured they would be suited perfectly for one another.

So, after folding her purple sheets and placing them carefully in her suitcase, off she went to her new room allocation, far from Elaine and her gang of bullies. Stepping out of Maroon for the last time was cathartic.

Admittedly, she always was something of a hothead. Or at least her mother always said so. And it was true; her emotions ran from hot to cold, sometimes quicker than expected. Sometimes her feelings ran *really* cold. That was how she had endured the final three days with her god-awful roommate until she could move.

"Here, kitty, kitty. Want some milk?" Diana had giggled, shaking a bottle of milk at her.

Well, joke was on them because she actually loved drinking milk. "Sure," she scoffed, grabbing the bottle of milk out of a very surprised Diana's hands as she stomped past them.

As much as she'd tried to save her dignity, she was still shaking mad when she finally made her way to Indigo Dorm.

If only someone could explain to her why she was accepted into this elite school only to be surrounded by shifters she couldn't relate to. Shifters who made fun of her. And why had her mother let her come here to be ridiculed?

Approaching Indigo C, she knocked on the door. Almost instantly, the door swung open, and a short and pretty Asian girl, possibly Korean, peeked out at her, beaming.

Ava's shoulders instantly relaxed, and she let out a breath she hadn't realized she was holding. The girl hadn't even spoken yet, but there was something reassuring in her big rounded eyes.

"Oh, hello! You must be Ava! I'm JiSoo. Come in, come in. We're going to have so much fun together!" JiSoo squealed. Thick accent—definitely Korean. She bent and lifted Ava's heaviest bag as if it were made of powder, and disappeared into the room.

Relieved she hadn't been allocated to stay with a new version of evil, Ava took a step inside. JiSoo had already pranced to the left side of the room to place Ava's suitcase on what Ava could only assume was her new bed. Then the girl announced, "This is your side. I know the bed's probably not as big as the one you had over at Maroon, but..." Then her already round eyes rounded even more—bulged, actually—and she pointed frantically at Ava's feet.

Ava jumped, afraid she was standing on a big cockroach or something, but when she looked down, she saw only the empty hardwood floor. But JiSoo continued pointing, waving her petite fingers in horror.

"What's wrong?" Ava looked back and forth frantically.

"No shoes in the room!" JiSoo was almost hyperventilating now. She gesticulated, her eyes bulging more as they opened wider.

Then something shocking and profoundly disturbing happened. Something Ava couldn't have been prepared for in a million years.

Her new roommate's eye popped right out of its socket and rolled underneath her bed. One look at the hole in JiSoo's face, and Ava's scream rocked the walls of their room.

"Your eye! Under... Bed... What the heck? Omigod! HELP! HELP!" Ava took several steps backward until she crashed into the door, panting like a dog.

"Oh my! I'm so sorry..." JiSoo squatted in front of the bed and reached under to retrieve her missing eyeball. She patted her tiny hand around underneath for a moment until she found it, wiped it off with her fingers, and popped it back in the socket.

Ava gagged immediately and had to swallow down her own vomit. "Holy mother of crap on a stick! You just shoved it in! Your eye... You just... Oh god..."

"But I don't need help. Look, I'm fine, see? No blood," JiSoo tried to comfort her. "Just calm down, please."

"But, but—but, seriously, what was that though? You scared the hell out of me!" Ava blustered.

"Just take off your shoes at the door, and I'll tell you." JiSoo pointed at Ava's feet again.

Without question this time, Ava slipped out of her black platform Mary Jane's, another gift from her mother, and then continued ranting, "These types of things should come with a warning label, you know?! You can't just go around giving people heart attacks. That's not okay. You need a sign on the door or something that says 'Warning, my eye may pop out—don't be alarmed!'"

JiSoo obviously found her reaction thoroughly amusing, but she didn't laugh out loud at least.

"I'm a pug shifter. It happens sometimes." She shrugged. "And by sometimes, I mean almost constantly."

A pug shifter? Okay, that made sense actually. Ava thought of Buster, her pug at home. It had only happened once before, but he had gotten startled, and yes, one of his eyes had indeed popped out of its socket. It just kind of dangled there on his face, and it was disgusting. Lucy had taken him to the vet to get it pushed back in. And Ava was very grateful she hadn't had to witness it.

"Okay then," Ava finally said. "So you're a pug shifter. All right, but I really should have been warned first thing. Come here, feel my heart! It's about to jump out, see?"

"Mmmhmm." JiSoo pressed her lips together and nodded. She certainly didn't come check to see if Ava's heart was actually about to jump out. "Yeah, so anyway, where's the rest of your stuff? Is this it?"

Ava examined her new roommate. JiSoo was small for her age, but not as much as the phoenix shifter. Her short-cropped black hair spiked out at the edges, showing off her thin neck and narrow shoulders. Her face was rounded, and her cheeks were cherub chubby. She wore a white crop top and denim overalls. They suited her. Ava looked down at her own plaid dress. She was still wearing her school uniform because she was in such a hurry to get out of Elaine's room as quickly as possible.

"Yes. I mean, no. I still have two bags waiting in the hall in Maroon. My friend was supposed to come help me with them but didn't show up in time. And I should probably go back for them before someone messes with them. Would you like to help?"

"Sure. I wasn't doing anything anyway." JiSoo just smiled brightly again, and Ava could swear she saw that right eyeball twitch, making her nervous.

JiSoo pranced over to the door next to Ava, her movements short and quick. Ava pulled her shoes back on as JiSoo slipped into hers. Together, they headed down the halls and took the whirling stairs. The staircase carried them over to Maroon Dorm, Ava's former hellhole.

On arriving at the hall that led to Ava's old room, they saw Winta struggling with the remaining two bags. "What took you so long?" Winta whined, dumping the bags back down on the floor.

"I'm sorry, but you didn't show up in time, and I was itching to get away from Elaine," Ava defended herself, crossing the hall to sling her arms around her best friend's shoulders. "This is my new room-mate, JiSoo, and she just scared the crap out of me. Do you know each other?"

"Oh, come on, it wasn't that bad," JiSoo objected. "Hi Winta, I've seen you around. You're the elephant shifter, right?" JiSoo bowed.

Winta quickly bowed back, bending low. She had to bend pretty far, considering JiSoo was at least a foot shorter. But by the time she stood back up, JiSoo bowed again, even lower this time.

So Winta did the same. So JiSoo bowed again.

Winta bowed one more time, and as JiSoo dipped again, Ava burst into laughter.

Winta stopped herself mid bow and straight-ened, looking at JiSoo quizzically. "You mean, mean girls," she said with a smile, obviously not really upset.

Elaine and her gang could be heard through the door, twittering in the room, so Ava motioned for them to get going. She didn't want to risk having to interact with any of them again or their onslaught of insults they'd definitely hurl at her and her friends. They already made fun of her for being a cat and having an elephant best friend. She could only imagine how they would handle a pug shifter with eyes that literally popped out of socket.

Between them, carrying the rest of the bags was much easier, and it took them only minutes to get back to Ava's new room in Indigo, which was conveniently only a few doors down from the room where Winta kept all her belongings.

In no time, all three girls were gathered around Ava's new closet, helping her sort out her clothes.

"So did you write that letter?" Winta asked, holding up a shimmery red dress against her own body in front of the mirror.

"That dress would look so good on you. Do you want to see if it fits? And no, I've been too busy fighting with Elaine and changing rooms." Ava stuffed several pairs of socks inside a drawer.

Winta hung the dress in the closet without trying it on.

"Excuse me? That sounds romantic! You have a crush?" JiSoo asked, clapping her hands a couple times.

"What? Oh, no. That's not it," Ava answered, silently asking Winta with her eyes if she thought it was okay to let JiSoo in on the information about her parents.

Winta nodded almost imperceptibly.

"It's a letter to my mother," Ava finished.

"Already homesick?" JiSoo tilted her head to the side as she held up a pair of Ava's panties on display.

"No!" Ava snatched her underwear away from JiSoo. Then she filled her in on the situation before JiSoo made more assumptions.

"I smell a mystery." JiSoo rubbed her hands together after Ava finished.

"Me too, actually," Winta agreed. "I've been thinking about it a lot since you first told me. It really is so mysterious."

"We could go back to the library," suggested Ava. "There's bound to be more on my father. We could microfiche all day."

"What's that?" Winta questioned her.

"It's like a TV, but we'll be slotting newspapers into it." Ava answered, a huge burden off her shoulders. These girls didn't judge that she was a tabby—didn't care. One an elephant, JiSoo a pug... Oh, she had her a group of misfits, that was for sure. And it made her smile.

Winta was also the first African friend she ever had and JiSoo the first Korean—a staunch one, no less, by the way she panicked when Ava wore her shoes into the room. And if she counted Tarun and James, that covered her first Indian and European friends. And here she was in Australia. She chuckled at the thought. There were a lot of different accents flying all around her nowadays. She wondered how odd her American accent sounded to everyone else.

"So what's your story, JiSoo? Why did your roomie leave?" Winta asked.

JiSoo froze, then stiffened her shoulders. Ava melted right then—she knew that gesture so well in this school. It came from having to defend what you were to others—every time.

"I'm a pug, so it got awkward..." she tossed at them, carefully arranging shoes by color. "The eye thing...it freaked her out. So when the attendants asked if anyone wanted to swap, she jumped at it, and I guess I don't blame her. I'd freak, too, if I were her. It's pretty weird."

"Well, she might not have thought it was that strange if she knew anything about pugs," Ava offered. "Sure, it surprised me, but now that I know, I can deal with it. We had to take my pug back home, Buster, to the vet for it as well. If someone can't accept you for who you are, screw them."

JiSoo relaxed back on her heels. "You guys really don't mind?"

"Mind?" Winta asked. "I kind of want to see it now..."

JiSoo laughed. "Well, I'm certainly not doing it on purpose! I'm sure it will happen around you soon enough if you spend enough time with me."

Winta grinned. "Fair enough."

"It really is just so embarrassing shifting into

someone's house pet though." JiSoo looked dejected again.

"You think I don't know how that feels?" Ava stood, walked to the center of the room, where the light could pour over her, and shifted into her tabby cat.

"Oh, you're adorable, Ava!" JiSoo made her hands into fists and waved them excitedly. "I remember you from the first day of school. I thought you were so cute."

Ava meowed warningly.

"Don't call her cute. She hates that," Winta said, stepping over to stroke her friend's furry back.

"Yeah, I guess I can totally understand that." JiSoo nodded.

A few moments later, Ava was standing in the middle of the room again, back in her human form.

"Now it's my turn," JiSoo offered.

Before anyone could object, not that they would have, the room filled with the sound of cracking bones and stretching sinew. Less than twenty seconds later, a fat, wrinkly little pug was running around in a circle on the rug, barking happily.

"Oh my gosh!" Ava yelped, dropping to her knees to hold her hands out to JiSoo. JiSoo ran to her and jumped into her arms. "You remind me of Buster! But much prettier!" She added that last part after JiSoo gave a little bark at her comment.

"What an interesting creature you turn into," Winta said slowly, eyeing JiSoo.

JiSoo turned her attention to Winta and trotted over to her. With hesitation, Winta reached her hand out carefully. JiSoo licked her palm, and Winta burst into a giggle fit.

Ava laughed, too. "Have you not seen a pug before?"

"No!" Winta was still giggling, and now JiSoo was running back and forth in front of her, wagging her tail and hamming it up. "We don't have them in Kenya. But now I see I've been missing out. What a splendid animal! Look at that wrinkly little face..." She grabbed the sides of JiSoo's cheeks and shook them.

Ava cringed inwardly, imagining how horrified she would be if someone did that to her in her cat form. But JiSoo didn't seem to mind at all. Instead, she sat back on her hind legs and wiggled her head back and forth, letting her wrinkles shake even more. *Wow, I can't believe this is really happening!*

. . .

After at least ten more minutes of JiSoo enter-taining Winta, she finally shifted back. "I'm so glad you enjoyed me as a pug!" she exclaimed. "Really, you don't even know how much that means to me."

"I wish I could return the favor right now," Winta told her. "But if I transform here, I would trash your room. So I'd rather not."

"Can I see your mark, at least?" JiSoo asked.

Winta lifted her right shirtsleeve to show off her shifter mark, barely visible against her dark skin.

"Wow," JiSoo whispered. "I bet you're the only elephant in the school, right?"

Winta nodded. "There haven't been many of us here in the last hundred years or so. The few who have attended here were all my family."

"I've got to see you."

"In due time, I'm sure. Just like you said about me getting to see your eyeball." She winked. "Let's finish helping Ava, and then, maybe, if there's time, we can head to the courtyard."

Together, they went back to arranging the new room setup and chattering excitedly. Ava didn't know it yet, but she just formed a small army. Ride-or-die friends who would be there for her no matter what.

And now, with genuine friends by her side, she had even more to distract her. In fact, she'd been so preoccupied in her search for anything concerning her father, being mad at her mother, and dealing with mean old Elaine, that she forgot about the very spectacular occurrence that had taken place in Professor Bills's class...

She could heal.

18

Tarun had two main skills. One was running, naturally, as he was a tiger, and the other was strumming his old guitar. His friends never ceased to compare his voice to Indian celebrities. As a little boy, he dreamed of playing in Bollywood movies. But, as he got older, he just liked to do it for fun.

That afternoon, sitting under an alcove of trees in the back courtyard, and surrounded by other students, he belted out some tunes until he eventually settled on the *Friends* theme song. It was one of his favorites.

His parents had loved that TV show, and he had watched every episode with them, eventually coming to love it, too. Playing that song on his guitar made him feel more connected to them and their favorite series.

"So no one told you life was gonna be this wayyyyy..."

Several other shifters joined in. "Your job's a joke, you're broke, your love life's DOAaaa..."

Then everyone who knew the song joined in for the chorus. "I'll be there for youuuu." At the end, he strummed a few more chords, then returned to the beginning.

Behind him, where no one could see her, Ava stood with JiSoo and Winta, her mouth hanging open. What in the universe did an alpha jock like Tarun see in a sappy show like *Friends*? She couldn't believe they had that weird little thing in common.

She could only see his back, and the way it arched over the guitar. His soulful heart-wrenching voice that somehow made the mundane theme song sound melodious, rang out through the trees. His white hair tickled the tops of his ears.

"That's the guy you like? Wow. Tarun. He's super hot." JiSoo broke the silence and snapped Ava from her stupor.

"I don't have a crush on him!" she insisted.

"Yes, that's her crush," Winta concluded as she elbowed Ava in the side playfully.

"Okay, maybe I kind of find him attractive... And I like his personality..." Ava answered, sounding a little dreamier than she meant to. It frustrated her that she couldn't approach him around all those people. It would be too embarrassing for both of them. Especially with so many predators in the vicinity.

The three girls had gone out to the courtyard together that afternoon so JiSoo could finally see Winta as an elephant.

They had already been there, done that, now, having retreated to the back woods behind the building, far from view of any wandering students.

Even Ava hadn't seen Winta shift very many times. They were separated for many classes, so Ava enjoyed watching the transformation almost as much as JiSoo. And Winta had done it slow and steady, just to make it extra dramatic. She started with giving herself a trunk, and then one foot, followed by the other. Then out came the ears, and after stomping around and trumpeting several times, she twirled in a circle until she eventually morphed fully.

As an elephant, Winta was truly an impressive sight to behold. Ava didn't think she would ever tire of seeing her do it. It was such a shame she was too embarrassed to do it in front of others. If only the other shifters weren't so cruel.

"Damn, girl, you got it bad!" JiSoo chimed in again, teasing Ava. This time imitating the face Ava was supposedly just making, mouth hanging open and all.

Ava elbowed her, and JiSoo squealed. The noise caught Tarun's attention, and he stopped singing and swiveled around to see what the ruckus was all about. As soon as he saw Ava standing there with her friends, his face broke into a big smile. He immediately waved them over.

"Don't even invite them over, Bro," Colin wheedled, his lips turning down at the sides, already getting up and brushing off the back end of his jeans. "I'm not hanging around."

Tarun pretended not to hear and continued waving. If anything, his wave got more exaggerated and his smile grew bigger.

He could clearly see the girls arguing, of course, and the minor scuffle taking place between them. Ava dragged her feet, flailing her hands, while Winta pushed her forward. Ava pulled her strands of brown hair in front of her face again, and Tarun really wished she wouldn't. It seemed like she always had her hair covering half of her face, and he wanted to see those rosy lips and catlike eyes more clearly. But, especially on the few occasions she tucked it behind her ears, her hair looked beautiful. Down almost to her waist and always parted in the middle.

Finally, the tiny dark-haired girl with them, JiSoo was her name, if Tarun's memory served him correctly, came bounding over to where he sat.

Giving in, Ava followed, with Winta giving her an occasional push behind the elbow. The scene was fairly comical to watch.

Patiently, he waited as he strummed a few nonsensical cords. James, who sat next to him, had just looked up to see the girls coming toward them. And, as expected, his face went from cool and collected to, well, looking like a blundering idiot again. A few others remained in the group as the girls approached, which Tarun appreciated. At least they were enjoying his music, and probably wouldn't give a rat's ass if they were all earthworm shifters.

As Ava moved toward him, he admired her slim figure, but tried not to stare. Her walk was unique, fluid and free, very feminine, especially in her heeled black boots.

She sat down beside him on the cobblestones,

her mates sitting on either side of her. "So you're a *Friends* fan? I wouldn't have guessed."

James immediately scooted closer to Winta.

"I think there's probably a lot you don't know about me..." Tarun started, leaning closer to Ava and trying to smile coyly at her.

But then a tiny hand poked him in the face. "Hi! I'm JiSoo." JiSoo extended her hand so abruptly that Tarun had leaned his face right into it at the same time.

"Right. JiSoo. I met you at the cafeteria a few weeks ago, yes?" He flashed her a charming smile.

"Oh yes! Yes, you did!" JiSoo seemed excited about that. "I didn't think you would remember me."

"Sure, of course I remember you. You have cool hair." He winked, but then immediately regretted it, worried Ava might see it and think he was flirting with her.

But Ava just smiled at their interaction, seemingly pleased that he was being so nice to her new friend.

"So what were the three of you ladies doing back there? Hiding from me and my god-awful singing voice?" he teased.

"Yeah, right." Ava sat there cross-legged with her back straight, twisting her unpainted finger-nails over and under each other on her lap. He wanted her to point those lovely doe-eyes on him. But the way they flashed, sometimes he couldn't tell if she was upset or amused.

"But I guess you couldn't resist all my awesomeness, so you still had to come over?"

He chuckled when she shot him a glare that could maim. "You wish," she blurted.

After a moment, he muttered softly, holding her eyes captive, "You've been avoiding me."

"Well, now I'm confused. I'm avoiding you or I can't resist you? Pick one." Was she trying to sound cute and flirtatious? Because it just came out catty. Yeah, pun intended.

"I haven't seen you since the library—"

"What's the deal with Levine?" Ava interrupted, changing the subject. "She's always by the door now every afternoon."

Tarun pretended not to notice the deliberate change in subject matter. "It's the best way for her to monitor the water shifters. Out of everyone, they are some of the most violent, and I guess they've been fighting a lot lately."

"The water shifters are more violent than the dragons?" JiSoo entered herself into the conversation.

"Yeah, overall. For the most part, the dragons don't try to devour each other." Tarun pointed.

"Just like those two are doing in the water right now!"

Ava broke their gaze right when he said it to turn and witness to silver sharks snapping viciously at each other. Alarmed, she said frantically, "Someone needs to stop them!"

"Oh, don't worry, that's nothing. They do this stuff all the time. Levine won't intervene until the water stains red."

"That's awful," Winta added, sounding surprised.

"Yeah, well, wait till you see what happens then." Tarun let out a low whistle. "You know sharks can't resist blood."

"Yes, I *do* know." Ava nodded her head emphatically. "Back home, I refused to swim at the beach for that exact reason. What if I had a cut on me and didn't know? They can catch the scent of blood from miles away! That's terrifying."

There were another several moments of silence while the group watched the shark shifters. Then Tarun spoke. "So, how have you been holding up? Elaine still giving you trouble?"

She cut him another incredulous look. "You really don't know?"

"Know what?"

"I had to change rooms. She made it impossible

to stay with her, threatened me, and then got me kicked out."

Tarun didn't know what to say so he didn't respond.

"But it all turned out for the better, because now I stay with JiSoo here." She nodded her head in JiSoo's direction. JiSoo was chattering animatedly with James and Winta.

Tarun felt immensely relieved for Ava. He knew Elaine was a nightmare and could probably make a person lose his or her mind. He also knew she had it out for Ava in a big way.

"I didn't even know it was possible to switch roommates! I wonder if Levine would let me do that so I could stay with James instead of Deacon..." he pondered aloud.

"Very doubtful." Ava shook her head. "I really don't want to tell you all the horrible things Elaine said about me to get the room switch to happen."

"Well, JiSoo seems nice."

"She *is* nice, just don't wear shoes in her room," she deadpanned.

He laughed and held out his hand as he moved to a kneeling position before standing up. "I'm Indian, I've been trained properly. I never wear shoes in someone's living space. Now, come with me?"

"Where we going?" She stood on her own without taking his hand.

He was going out on a limb here, but he was glad she was going with it. "You'll see."

———————

Curiosity. Blame it on her curiosity. It always got the best of her.

"Winta, JiSoo, I'll be back soon, okay?"

JiSoo had the gall to wink outrageously at her and even make kissing sounds.

"Stoooooopppp!" Ava tried to say to her so only JiSoo could hear, but she didn't know if she was successful. She was about ready to throw her new roomie through a pug-sized hole in the wall.

Thankfully, Winta, friend that she was, back-handed JiSoo in the stomach.

Thank you, Winta.

Still glaring at JiSoo as she followed Tarun, they took off down the cobblestone path. Wondering where he was taking her, she tried to crush the butterflies filling her insides. Walking behind him didn't make them go away. Instead, her eyes were glued to his backside—er, ahem —*pants*. Yes, his plaid uniform pants. On most of the boys there, she thought those pants looked horrendous and ridiculous. Like a bunch of clowns waltzing around. But on him they were, well, kind of cool looking. She could see the tails of his shirt poking out from below his blazer.

She took a deep breath and grasped for something to say. Anything to distract herself right now. Finally, "I'm dying of curiosity. Seriously, where are we going? I've never been this far away from the school building."

He merely chuckled and reached for her hand. When she finally took it, after about ten seconds of hesitation, he said, "Careful now. Curiosity killed the cat, you know." He winked flirtatiously.

Ava tried to roll her eyes as dramatically as possible. "Oh, please, very original. Like I haven't heard that a million times!" *Even though my curiosity gets me into trouble all the time,* Ava did not say.

As they came to a grassy field, the school was now a blur from that distance. "I'm so confused about this school's location," Ava admitted. "At first, I thought the school was underground. And then I thought it wasn't. But then I was told it was, and all this stuff is just a glamour. But how are we under skies that I can very much feel the breeze from, hearing the ocean that I can also feel a breeze from and smell the salt, and now we are walking on a grassy field? This is grass! Definitely grass."

Tarun gave her a weird look. "That's what's bothering you? We're at Animage Academy. There are people who can turn to jellyfish and three-toed sloths here. Our headmistress is a mythical beast, and you watched a girl burn to death in class only to explode into a magical firebird."

"Yes. So?"

"So I'm just saying, it's not entirely impossible for the school to create an atmosphere suitable for human and other mammal habitation."

"But we're underground. Standing on grass. Looking at the sky."

"You look so confused. It's cute." He squeezed her hand. "Headmistress Levine's family has been here since the onset of the school. That was like a thousand years ago or something insane like that. Ava? Are you listening?"

Omigod! He said she was cute! She could probably die happy now. *Wait, what did he say?* "What?"

He laughed at her. *Oh crap.* She definitely missed something.

"I was talking about the origins of the school. Griffins are magical creatures, and they've been running the place since the beginning. They have all kinds of powers we can't even fathom nowadays because most of it has died off. Levine is the oldest living griffin left that we know of. There are only a handful of phoenixes, and unicorns are extinct now. So aside from the handful of other mythicals, and the legends I've heard about some human mages out there, there isn't much magic left. But it still exists."

"What about vampires and werewolves?" Ava asked him. She'd heard a lot of horror stories about them.

"Well, okay, I guess that's magic, too. But it's really different. They can't cast spells or create magical barriers or heal people." He scratched under his chin as he considered the possibilities. "I've always kind of figured they came from magic though. They wouldn't exist otherwise. But it must've been some kind of crazy dark magic, because getting bitten by one of them is a curse that ruins your life forever."

"Can shifters even become werewolves or vampires?" Ava questioned. "That seems a little weird."

"Oh, sure, it's definitely possible." Tarun nodded his head once. "I knew a shifter back in India who got attacked by a vampire. It was terrifying. He tried to fight the urge to feed, but eventually, the bloodlust got to him. He ended up putting a stake through his own heart."

Ava's hand shot to her mouth. "That's horrible!"

"Sure is." He looked away, but then spoke again. "Werewolves are even more common in the shifter community. Because if you think about it, it's easier for them to be trusted at first. They usually go for the wolf packs. Now there are entire werewolf packs. From there, they go for other shifters. But not all of them are bad, they just need to be contained during the full moon is all."

Ava was nodding along as Tarun spoke. This was fascinating. But then suddenly, something he'd said earlier struck her. "When you mentioned magic, you mentioned healing?"

Tarun stopped walking and gaped at her. "Yes, I did."

Ava had a feeling he was thinking the same thing she was. He was thinking about her sudden healing ability in the training room right after she scratched herself open.

"So it's a magical ability then? So why..."

"I have no idea, but I was definitely wondering the same thing when it happened." He started walking again, and Ava fell in step beside him. "It doesn't make any sense for a tabby cat to be able to heal. Unless there's some sort of rare breed of magical tabby cats out there that no one has discovered yet." He laughed uncomfortably.

"I guess," Ava muttered, not sure what else to say.

"But anyway," Tarun went on. "The griffins... They are...special."

"How do you mean?"

"Griffins have special guardian powers. You could call them sorcerers, I guess. It allows them to break reality to suit their needs. In this case, to the taste of the school. It's fairly restrictive though, from what I understand. Their powers only benefit the place they are assigned to guard. So that's why Animage has thrived underground for so long undetected by humans."

"Wow! See, these are the kinds of lessons I'd love to be learning in class. Not just constant training." Ava added a little hop in her step. "I mean, I had pretty much no idea Levine was so cool."

"What, you thought she just stood around watching students all day? Filing her nails and doling out punishments?" he teased her.

Ava grinned, and they laughed together. She enjoyed his laugh, appreciating his deep baritone. "What about family? Does she have any? Of her own, I mean?"

"She does. A nephew, I think. And two sisters."

"You know so much about her family."

"Well, remember, my parents went here. She was here when they were here, too," he reminded her. "And last year, Deacon, Colin, Elaine, Michaela, and I, along with a bunch of others, spent over a week touring the school and learning about it. Colin knew a lot about her. He claimed he was related to her."

"School tour? That was an option?"

"Yeah, didn't you get an invite?"

"No, all I got was the acceptance letter."

Tarun slapped his palm to his forehead. "Oh, duh."

Ava clammed up. "Right. Because I'm just a tabby cat, so no one knew I would be coming here. There was no reason to invite me."

"I wasn't trying to be mean." His face looked genuinely apologetic. "But it's kind of the truth. James didn't get an invitation either. I never thought he'd be able to come here with me until that acceptance letter showed up only a few weeks before the semester started. We were all shocked."

"I guess whoever enacted the new policy did it very last minute." Ava dragged her feet a little more. "That's my life. This entire time I've been wondering why I was accepted. I'm a worthless little kitty cat. A noncombatant shifter from America. What the heck am I doing here?"

They had stopped walking again. Tarun looked into her eyes. "It wasn't just you though. They admitted people everywhere. But it's not like they admitted all shifters. They selected a group of you. The question is why."

Ava looked around. The school was almost

invisible now. She rubbed her palms over her goosebumped arms and blew out a deep breath. It came out in a white fog.

"You're cold," Tarun observed, taking off his blazer. "Here, take my jacket."

"I'm not even going to argue, I'm so cold," Ava admitted, snatching the blazer from his lax fingers.

Although now Ava had an additional problem. Tarun's arms were visible because he was no longer wearing the blazer. The boys kept their shirt sleeves rolled up pretty far at all times, to keep their marks visible, so his muscles bulged. Ava could swear his biceps were calling to her. And that beautiful dark skin...from his year-long tan, deliciously browned. She could bite them...

Shaking her head vigorously, she shrugged the jacket on. It smelled just like him. A woody, earthy scent that was all male. Ava pretended to adjust the sleeves so she could inhale the fragrance deeply. Then her hair snagged on one of the buttons as she tried to drag it down.

Yup, he was about to lose all respect for her any second now. Apparently she couldn't even dress herself without screwing it up.

She pulled at her hair, hurting herself, and trying to get it detangled before he noticed. But luckily, he was distracted by something, turned around and facing the other way. She was thankful he couldn't see her head bent in that awkward position.

"We're here," he announced suddenly, turning in that very unfortunate moment to see her wrestling her hair away from the button.

Damn long hair!

"Here, let me help with that," he said sweetly. He didn't laugh at her or make fun of her or anything.

Within seconds, he had freed her from her tangled mess.

And what did he mean when he said they were "here"? They were literally in the middle of nowhere, standing in a wide expanse. The clouds dipping low, rocks jutting from the ground. She had to concentrate very hard not to trip over one in her boots.

Gently, he pushed her long hair back over her shoulder, far away from the button in question. That left him standing close. Too close. She could feel his hot breath on her face, even hear his heart pounding. Or was that hers?

Her breath hitched in her throat at the sight of his deep green eyes so near her own. Then his lashes swept down, shielding her from seeing what was in their depths. Unconsciously, her right hand trailed up his brawny arms, tracing his musculature.

He gasped softly, nearly inaudibly.

It was the last thing she heard—last thing she remembered—before he lowered his head to hers.

His lips, so silky and smooth, on hers surpassed anything she'd imagined. She felt like her head had just exploded in a burst of light the second his mouth touched hers. She'd kissed boys before, but nothing more. And nothing, at all, came even close to this mass of electricity surging through her charged body.

He was gentle but driving her crazy, with little nips on her lower lip, teasing them open and then tickling them with his tongue. Gladly, she welcomed his tongue in the rest of the way, a sigh escaping when she did so.

Someone groaned. She wasn't sure if it came from her or Tarun.

She pushed closer, wanting to feel every inch of him. Her fingers, completely out of her control, traveled up his firm arms, over his shoulders, to his neck, and finally delved into his hair. Oh, that hair was even softer to touch than she'd hoped.

She moaned again, a little louder this time. His tongue explored every part of her mouth, plunging, enjoying. He gave as much as he took, and she matched his every move. His hands on her waist held on like it was the only thing holding him to the ground.

His fingers trailed over her back, and she couldn't help it—she moaned into his mouth. The sound was a wake-up call, and Ava suddenly had an alarming thought. She wrenched her mouth and hands away from him and took several steps backward.

She knew he was dangerous, but not to this extent.

How dare he.

He knew his confusion was stamped boldly across his face as he struggled to regain his breath. He'd thought they were on the same page, but she was now looking at him as if he were the fungus that grew beneath the earth's surface.

"Is that why you brought me here? Just so you could take advantage of me?"

"What? Ava! No!" He was so utterly shocked that he didn't even know for sure if his words had been decipherable. His original intention had been to get her out here so they could practice partial cat-shifts together at a cool little cave he'd found, but he just couldn't resist her.

"Tell me it isn't true." She looked furious.

Stunned into silence, he could only watch her as she fumed. Rage had completely replaced the passion he was so sure had just consumed *both of them* only moments ago.

"You can't, can you? That's what I thought," Ava spat. She hurriedly unbuttoned the jacket, untucked her hair where it was caught inside the collar, and chucked it back at him.

He didn't even try to catch it—it just hit him in the face. He opened his mouth, but then closed it again. He wanted to explain, to exonerate himself, but he didn't even know how to do that. And his brain was still a little foggy from their passionate kiss.

What the heck? Hadn't she felt it, too?

Wasn't she tingling from head to toe, even now, like he was?

He could only watch in astonishment as she stormed away, making sure not to look back at him. He briefly considered going after her, to keep her from assuming the worst about him, but considering how quickly things had turned, he didn't know how he would convince her otherwise.

Instead, he stood, glued to the spot as he watched her until she was a tiny speck running toward the school.

19

Winta was unclipping her earrings when Ava barged into her room without knocking.

"We gotta go." Ava appeared a bit feverish, but Winta tamped down the urge to test her friend's temperature with the back of her hand.

"Go where?"

"To the library. Hurry."

Winta totally, with all her heart, disagreed with Ava about needing to go there. She wasn't going to the library in the middle of the night. An elephant needed her beauty rest.

"I don't know what's gotten into you, but please sit down and tell me what's going on. Something tells me we don't really need to go anywhere right now," Winta cajoled, subtly craning her neck to see if JiSoo was behind her, in on this crazy plan.

Nope, she was nowhere near. She was probably in her own room, nestled under her sheets—like a normal person—dead to the world.

Ava started moving from one end of her room to the other, too fast to be considered pacing.

Thankfully, Winta's "roommate," Michaela, was out with her friends, so she didn't have to witness any of this.

"I can just tell you on the way." Ava's words tumbled quickly, just like her feet. Winta could feel her floor moving underneath Ava's footsteps. Impressive for a kitten.

She took a deep breath and set her earrings down in her jewelry box. She had to point out the obvious. "The library is closed, Ava. Let's say I do go with you now. How exactly do you intend to get in without being noticed?"

Ava stopped—thankfully—and stared at her, crossed and uncrossed her arms, and then made a couple noises that weren't really words. She hadn't even bothered with real clothes, standing there in her polka-dot nightwear. "We'll just figure it out when we get there. I need to see something, Winta. Please, come with me."

"We'll go in the morning. First thing, will that work? Just please stop running all over the place!

You're making me dizzy." Winta was used to her friend's back-and-forth temperaments, but it didn't mean she enjoyed them.

The semi-insane look dissipated from Ava's eyes as she padded over to the bed and sat down. The bed that would be Winta's if it weren't for her sleep-shifting. Curling up into a ball, Ava looked small and vulnerable. "But I just want to know if I'm right. This will clear up so many things for me."

Winta let out a little cough to cover her sigh. At least they were getting somewhere. And now the risk of being expelled for breaking into the library at this hour was reducing somewhat.

She leaned in closer to her friend, scooting her chair several inches. Then she moved the curtain of brown hair shadowing Ava's face and reached for her hand. But she nearly dropped it as soon as she touched it because Ava's hands were ice cold. That's when she realized Ava was shivering. "Ava? What's going on? You know you can tell me anything..."

"I couldn't sleep and I... I just remembered something earlier." She shrugged noncommittally.

"Yes?" Winta prompted. She had expected Ava to dish out all the details from her afternoon "walk" with Tarun, but this was clearly a different matter entirely.

"Suffice it to say..." Ava trailed off, seemingly

changing her mind about what she was about to tell her. "You see, I cut myself in class the other day. When I was doing some partial shifting."

"Oh no. You didn't tell me about that. Poor thing. Can I see?"

"No, you can't, actually. That's the problem." Ava lifted her polka-dot sleeve. "It was right here, but it's totally gone. See?"

Winta looked over her arm. Indeed, she didn't see a single scratch. "Are you sure you cut yourself? I mean, was it just minor?"

"Oh, I'm definitely sure." Ava's eyes were wide. "There was blood *everywhere*, and it was super painful. I had my claws out, and it just went so deep...I..."

"Just take a breath," Winta coaxed her. She was worried Ava was about to get hysterical.

"It happened that day in Professor Bills's class. The same day he mentioned my father. But I completely forgot about it because I was so distracted with the fact my father went to the school. Then, on my walk with Tarun yesterday, he mentioned—"

Winta raised an eyebrow. "That walk with Tarun? You seriously aren't going to tell me how that went?"

"You just gotta come with me! I need to see if

there are answers in the library!" Ava's breathing grew erratic again.

Winta abandoned the subject of Tarun. "Seriously, just breathe. Relax and think about this because I don't think you have. Like *at all*. Say we go down there... We get caught, then we get sent back home. You and I never see each other again. You never see Tarun again. Or JiSoo. You don't find your father and you never get answers. Then what?" Winta noticed she was talking too fast, but she was past caring. She wanted to talk sense into Ava, and Ava should be used to her accent by now.

Ava's hand that Winta was holding slackened, and she threw herself backward on the carefully made bed. A plume of dust flew up around her, causing her to make her face. No one really used that bed because Winta still slept outside. She really only used it to lay out her clothes in the evenings.

"Do you know what this means?"

When Winta didn't answer, Ava went on, "That I'm freakier than I thought. Apparently it isn't enough that I'm a *wittle kitty.*"

"Don't say that."

"But it's true. Apparently my cuts heal for no reason at all."

"Has that always been the case though?" Winta reached out and touched her friend's hand again.

Surely someone would have noticed that she healed instantly. "What about when you were a child? I'm sure you fell from trees and things like that."

Ava chuckled. "Are you kidding me? It's my cat nature. I used to climb trees all the time and then get stuck!"

Winta had to laugh at that as well. Of course Ava did that.

"But I bruised myself and cut myself up all the time. Just like any regular kid would. I never healed instantly."

"Not until you got here."

"That's right. Not until I got here."

Winta had a thought. "How old were you when you started to manifest?"

Ava looked at her. "My shifting abilities? Twelve. You know, pretty typical."

"And how old were you before you could shift fully?"

Ava's face turned slightly red. "Honestly? My first full shift—like, *on purpose*—was only about a month before I came here," she said quietly.

Winta nodded. "So maybe this healing ability took a while to manifest as well. Like your shifting ability. Maybe they're related."

"But tabby cats don't heal on command!" Ava waved her hands. "I don't know why, but I really believe this has something to do with my father. He's the only blank sheet in my life. Maybe finding him would explain all this."

"Well, I can definitely understand why you couldn't sleep," Winta reassured her.

Looking suddenly shy, Ava said, "Um, something else happened, too."

Finally! Ava was going to tell her about Tarun. "Oh, that doesn't sound good. Don't tell me an attendant saw you taking off clothes or something..."

"Oh god, no! Nothing like that. He just walked me really far out to the fields..."

"I know. I saw the two of you walk out there together. Remember?"

"Mmmhmm, yeah, so there's that... And so we kissed..."

"Ohhhhh!" Winta squealed. Ava rushed to cover her mouth with her palm to shush her, probably expecting the hallway attendant to push open their door at any moment. Winta pushed her hand away.

"Yes, he kissed me." But then Ava bit her lip. "It just kind of happened. One minute he was untangling his jacket from my hair, and the next, he was kissing me..."

"I'm trying to follow this story, but so many things don't add up."

"Ugh! I totally screwed it up. I had to stop it. It was just too much."

Winta was feeling completely lost now. "So you stopped him from kissing you? But you said he kissed you. So did you stop him after? I'm so confused."

Bringing her hands to cover her face, Ava grumbled, "It was too much. It occurred to me he was just using me. He dragged me all the way out there... Just to get me alone, and... Why else would a boy invite you off where no one can see you, and then make a move on you? Am I right?"

Winta's heart sank. She almost didn't want to know the rest of the story, but she kept quiet. Instead, she simply asked, "So what did you do?"

After about ten seconds of awkward silence, Ava grumbled, "I pushed him away, gave him a piece of my mind, and then stormed off."

Winta groaned louder than she meant to.

"He didn't even try to stop me," Ava went on. "He just stood there like a wounded animal, watching me rant, and then just let me go. I guess he didn't even care. Probably because he knew I was right."

There was no way Ava really believed that. Winta knew she was just saying the words to convince herself they were the truth. "Ava..."

"Don't start!" Ava snapped. "On top of all that,

he mentioned something about mythical shifters with magical abilities. One of them is the magical ability to heal."

Winta nodded her head. She hadn't thought of that. But her parents had read her stories about fabled shifters who could heal people and even bring them back from the dead.

"So now that's all I can think about," Ava finished.

But now Winta's head was spinning as well. That was a fascinating detail. Was there some sort of magical cat shifter out there? Maybe there was a lot more to Ava than any of them realized. Biting down on her lip, she looked at her friend. "We've already wasted time. Let's get to the library."

Elaine was on her way to Black Dorm. To Colin's room specifically. He'd called her over, and apparently Deacon and a few of the others were already there. She'd heard about Deacon's falling out with Tarun and wanted to help console him.

Who was she kidding... Console?

Nah.

She just wanted to go over there and complain about Tarun while the other attractive boys doted all over her.

It was pure coincidence that she saw the stupid cat and her elephant friend backing out of the Indigo hallway. What were they doing out at this hour? Both girls had to duck from the nighttime attendant patrolling the halls. Of course, she had to do the same, and jumped behind a pillar.

Elaine waited until the attendant was out of sight and the girls started on the move again before she followed stealthily behind them, being careful not to make a sound. She was interested to know why her goody-two-shoes former room-mate had decided to leave the comfort of her room to skulk around at night with her pesky friend.

At one point, she had to dodge behind a cleaning cart to keep from being seen. Then, as they neared Gold, she choked at the thought that perhaps Ava was stupid enough to visit her boyfriend in his dorm. She knew Tarun was alone in there because Deacon was at Colin's. But, to her relief, the girls sailed right past that wing as if it wasn't there and continued down the whirling stairs.

Sneaking down the stairs behind them was trickier because the steps creaked when they moved. She had to hang back at the top and wait for the girls to make it to the bottom before she shifted into her eagle as quietly as possible and, in one smooth movement, sailed down to the lower level to catch up with them.

It turned out they were headed to the library. Not at all what she'd been expecting, but now that she thought about it, it made sense. Ava had been skulking around the library the last time she caught her with Tarun. What could possibly be so important in that gross dusty room for her to risk expulsion?

The girls disappeared into the library and closed the door behind them. Elaine entertained the thought of barging into the room after them to expose them, but she knew that wouldn't go well for her either because she was also out of her room after hours. Instead, she tiptoed over to the doorway, still in her eagle form, and leaned up against the door to listen, utilizing her bird hearing once again to eavesdrop.

From her position, desperately hoping no one would walk by, she could hear everything they said. So the kitty's father abandoned her? It seemed fitting, Elaine thought. Who would want a pathetic daughter like Ava?

Oh, but there was more.

Her healing abilities. Now that was interesting. Elaine had caught wind of some commotion during training that day, but she hadn't fully grasped what happened. Apparently Ava's horrific wound had healed within seconds? What could that be about?

But as she stood and pondered those two details, mention of something else snapped her back to attention. That little brat had kissed Tarun?

Oh, she was going to make her suffer. After everything that stupid cat had put her through, Elaine would make her pay. And now she had even more information on her. She was stupid to sneak out with her friend.

Elaine had heard enough, and she moved away from the door. It appeared she'd have to take a little detour to Headmistress Levine's office.

20

The bright side of being a small fish in a huge pond was that no one ever paid you much attention. If you're too small to be seen, it's easy to sneak around.

Okay, so that turned out to be a lie. Sure, Ava was small. Sure, the academy was big. But she got way more attention than she wanted, and it turned out, sneaking around was not a luxury she could afford.

Here she had been so caught up in finding out more about her father and her healing abilities, that she'd thrown caution to the wind.

She whined, begged, and cajoled her friend into breaking the school rules and accompanying her to the library.

Upon entering the library, they had made their way through the dusty pages for about twenty minutes before Winta's head snapped up and looked around. Winta had been the smart one and thought to utilize her elephant hearing while they were in there.

"Someone's coming." Winta snapped the book she was holding closed with a smack and shoved it back on the shelf.

"Oh no! What should we do?" Ava felt like a deer in headlights.

Winta figured they could climb out one of the large gilded windows and jump into the bushes outside.

Filled with an urgency that spiked by the second, Ava clambered over the sill behind her friend.

She looked out the window, grateful she always landed on her feet because that was a pretty big drop. Winta was already on the ground below her, looking up with scared eyes. "Hurry!" How Winta had landed so gracefully without hurting herself, Ava had no idea. Maybe she shifted to her elephant feet as she landed or something?

Ava threw her legs over and jumped down, landing roughly on all fours. Before she could straighten back up, a bright light flashed onto her.

Coming to a full standing position, she and

Winta turned to stare directly into two very bright flashlights.

The end.

Or so it seemed. Perhaps, if everything really had ended outside the library with Headmistress Levine glaring at them, that probably would have been better. But no. It got worse.

Elaine, of all people, stood proudly beside the headmistress. She was the one holding the second flashlight.

"You girls better have an excellent explanation for this." There was no trace of humor in Levine's voice. Of course not.

Instead of responding, Ava and Winta simply stared back, still looking like deer in headlights.

Sighing, Levine tried again. "You know the rules, yet you chose to leave your rooms at this ungodly hour and break into the library? What was so important that couldn't wait until tomorrow?"

Ava couldn't seem to find her ability to talk. She wanted to make up some kind of lie, but her lips just wouldn't move. It appeared that Winta couldn't talk either. Ava felt tremendously guilty for dragging her friend into this.

"Elaine, that will be all. You should hurry to the

infirmary now." Levine waved Elaine off. "Now, as for the two of you..."

So that was how Elaine kept from getting in trouble for also sneaking out. Ava knew full well that Elaine hadn't been headed to the infirmary at that hour, but she had probably been such a quick thinker she came up with that story at the last second. Clever, actually.

Elaine scampered out...and did she give them the finger over her shoulder? Ava couldn't be sure, but she thought so. Of course, she couldn't be sure of anything when she was being dragged to the terrifying griffin's office.

Headmistress Levine forced them to stay the night in her office. Apparently that was also where the headmistress lived, and she disappeared through a doorway behind her desk. Intermittently, Levine had come in to check on them, but otherwise left them alone.

It was a very odd and unexpected punishment. Ava had no idea what she was going to do with them.

Neither of them slept a wink. Ava was too nervous to sleep, and even though Winta was probably also nervous, she also knew falling asleep and accidentally shifting would wreck Levine's beautiful little office.

"Good morning, ladies." The headmistress greeted them as she glided into the office as if she hadn't just kept them captive there half the night.

"Good morning," they both grumbled suddenly from her couch.

Levine strolled to her uncluttered desk to retrieve her purse, leaving the girls in suspense.

"What now?" Winta whispered to Ava as she uncurled herself from the couch. They only had a short time before breakfast, and Ava was definitely hungry, but she was still trying hard not to panic. Were they getting expelled or not?

Finally, Headmistress Levine returned; this time her hair and makeup looked neater. "You may go."

Ava just sat there and blinked. "That's it? We can just—"

"Yes," Levine cut her off. "I just spoke with Professor Bills, and I would like to speak with you in five days. I will call for you when it's time. But for now, you may go to breakfast and then head to class as usual."

Ava couldn't even believe this was happening. What was the headmistress getting at? They were seriously just going to strut right out of there with no punishment? Or was there a worse punishment coming? And five days? What was that all about? What would happen then?

"Don't just sit here and stare at me. I'm happy to come up with another punishment right now if you so desire," Levine warned.

"No, no!" Winta grabbed Ava's hand and pulled her up. "We're going. Thank you, Ma'am."

Ava followed Winta out of the office.

"You were right, that was a terrible idea. It's all my fault and I'm so sorry," Ava apologized. "I shouldn't have dragged you into my drama, I—"

"Stop talking, Ava, before you make it worse. I chose to go with you because I'm your best friend, and that's what we do. We stick by each other no matter what." Winta gave Ava's hand a tight squeeze.

Hand in hand, they returned to Indigo Dorm. Ava walked Winta to her room before retreating to her own. They got more than a few stares on their way, probably because they both looked like such a mess from sitting up all night.

Before Ava had even stepped one foot inside her room, JiSoo was in her face, bouncing up and down to make herself closer to Ava's height. "Why didn't you say anything?" the girl demanded, banging the door closed behind Ava.

JiSoo was already dressed for school, her uniform perfectly ironed, and her short cropped hair pulled awkwardly into two puffy pigtails that glinted in the light. Her hair was too short to fit entirely into the pigtails, so chunks stuck out all over.

"You were asleep. I didn't want to disturb you," Ava said matter-of-factly.

"Disturb me? You didn't even think to invite me out to wherever it was you went? Now, I've missed out on all the fun!" She stomped her little foot.

What? "Exactly what fun are you referring to? Winta and I almost got expelled!"

"Oh, so you could invite Winta, but not me?" JiSoo stamped her fists onto her hips in defiance. "Winta, who you had to go find. But not me, who was asleep right next to you!"

"It's not like that..."

JiSoo prodded Ava's chest with her tiny index finger. Ava was concerned those eyes could pop out at any second. They were bulging dangerously out of their sockets.

"We snuck into the library because I was desperate for more information about my father and his potential magical healing abilities. But we got caught, okay?"

JiSoo's eyes got even bigger. "I could've helped!

I would've gotten you into the library no problem. That's one thing I'm good at—"

"Actually, you just would've ended up on the headmistress's list along with us. Elaine ratted us out, and that's why we got caught." Ava kicked off her shoes and stepped into the room, figuring she could squeeze in a shower and still make it for the tail end of breakfast. Her roommate, on the other hand, had different ideas.

"You take your time getting ready," JiSoo offered. "I'm headed to the breakfast hall, and I can bring yours back."

"That would be wonderful, JiSoo, thank you so much." Ava meant it. She really wasn't ready to deal with everyone quite yet.

Without another word, JiSoo disappeared, off to fetch breakfast, and, not long after, Ava let out a sigh of satisfaction when she stepped into the hot shower.

When Ava exited of the bathroom, Winta was sitting on her bed. "JiSoo stopped in my room and told me to meet you here, and that she would bring us all breakfast?" Winta said it as more of a question.

Ava chuckled. "She's the best. If not kind of a lot to handle sometimes."

Just as she said that, the door flew open, and in pranced JiSoo with heaping trays of food in her hands. Kicking off her shoes, she brought the trays over and sat them down on the table in the corner. "Here you go, ladies! You're going to need this. You might want to brace yourselves for a lot of gossip."

"Great," Winta mumbled as she stuffed a pastry into her mouth.

"How did word even get out so quickly?" Ava picked up a piece of sausage.

"Elaine, I think," JiSoo explained. "People were talking very loudly. It sounded like the two of you robbed a bank or something."

"What about Tarun?"

"Yeah, he was there, too. And not so happy either." JiSoo bounced from one foot to the other. She really was a bouncy little thing. "How did Elaine catch you, anyway?"

"Beats me," Ava said. "I didn't even see her follow us, and the door to the library was closed while we were in there."

"Sounds to me like she has it out for you even more than you realize."

Ava just nodded as she took a bite of her eggs. "Flerfinflifsmo bufamotmosofmy."

"You might want to swallow the food in your mouth first," Winta suggested.

Ava took a big awkward swallow, and then repeated herself: "I guess so, but I don't know why."

JiSoo looked serious for a moment. "Just so you know, she's telling everyone about how your father abandoned you."

Ava's mouth fell open. She thought she felt a little piece of food fall down her shirt. "She knows about that?"

"That she does, and she isn't mincing words."

"What else did she say in this very enlightening breakfast conversation?"

"I don't know because I wasn't right next to her for all of it, but I did see Tarun stand up to yell at her. You should've seen her face go different colors in seconds. But it worked. She shut up after that."

"Tarun defended me?" Ava brought her hands up, wiggling a piece of bacon. "Why didn't you lead with that?"

"Why didn't you invite me along?" JiSoo moved her head back and forth.

Ava only smiled at that. She really appreciated JiSoo.

After scarfing down breakfast, the three girls stepped out of the dorm room together. As soon as Ava stepped into the hallway, she finally realized the full effects of their adventure.

Everywhere she looked, someone was pointing at them and whispering. Although she was fairly used to that, this was different—there was more open malice on the students' faces. JiSoo must have sugarcoated her version of the story for them somewhat.

It seemed that everyone had concluded she had broken into school property and stolen something. The shifters literally cleared a path for her as she and her friends walked by. When they got to the stairs, those cleared as well. No one would look directly at her for more than a split second. And conversations hushed when she got close by.

She thought it should have been obvious that she hadn't stolen anything, considering she was still there at the school. Yes, Levine had gone easy on her, for whatever reason, but she certainly would not have had she caught them stealing.

All Ava could do was square her shoulders and lift her chin and continue to class as if nothing was wrong.

As a few of the dolphins loudly made fun of her as they passed, JiSoo whispered to her, "Just ignore them. This will blow over as soon as they find someone else to pick on."

But she only listened to JiSoo with one ear. The other ear was busy listening to the jeering dolphins.

Thankfully, today's first class would have all the first-years together, so Winta and JiSoo stayed by her side.

21

At the door to the classroom, Ava collided with someone, and her bag slipped from her shoulder, spilling the contents all over the floor.

"Hey, Tabby, why don't you pay attention to your surroundings?" A pair of stiletto pumps stepped on the books and papers scattered on the floor. Elaine. In all her malicious glory. She grinned from ear to ear, her pink lipstick shining. Lashes thick with black mascara, and her studded jewelry making her hands and fingers sparkle.

Ava tried to ignore her and squatted down to pack her belongings back into her bag. JiSoo and Winta dropped to help her as well.

"What's the matter? Cat got your tongue?" Elaine's voice was syrupy sweet. Her flock, standing nearby, found her stupid comment hilarious and giggled uncontrollably.

Ava rolled her eyes. Everyone thought they were so clever with their cat jokes. But most of them weren't even remotely original.

"Excuse us. We're stepping through," Winta said to Elaine as she made to step past her. Elaine let her get by, but then stepped in front of Ava. JiSoo had apparently already snuck into the room —she was nimble like that.

"And what if I don't let you by?" Elaine sneered.

Out of all the things Ava needed in her life right at that moment, this was definitely not on the list. And it didn't help that there was a bottleneck of shifters forming behind her, waiting to enter the class. They were all starting to grumble and loudly complain, but that didn't discourage Elaine.

Ava wouldn't give all the onlookers the satisfaction of her making a scene, so she just said to Elaine quietly, "Haven't you done enough?"

Elaine leaned in closer. "I don't even know how you haven't been expelled yet, but I'm just getting started, Sweetie. When I'm done with you, you will wish we never met."

Ava rolled her eyes again. This time, she made sure Elaine could see it. "I already wish that, Elaine." With that, she ducked under Elaine's arm, inhaling the choking scent of Chanel No.7, and sailed into the classroom, headed straight for her favorite seat in the back.

Winta and JiSoo were already seated, and there were three empty seats next to them.

Ava settled in next to Winta as Levine's words echoed in her mind: "We pride ourselves on being the best, not just as shifters, but as dignified members of society. We can't have our students breaking rules. You broke in to the library, I assume for materials which are forbidden, and now you refuse to tell me why."

That was the lecture the headmistress had given them as she angrily escorted them to her office.

What exactly was it that was keeping Ava from sharing her reasons with the headmistress? Maybe she should have just admitted she was looking for information about her father. But for whatever reason, she felt the need to keep it a secret. And she was thankful Winta had her back.

When class started, she scanned the students for her favorite head of white hair. But he wasn't there. *Strange.*

She'd never seen him miss class. She entertained the thought that perhaps he heard all those things about her and decided to avoid her. In which case, Elaine's plan worked perfectly. But she had to remind herself that made little sense because he wouldn't skip class just to avoid her.

Throughout the lesson, Ava forced her brain to focus on the words floating around on the pages of *History of Shifter Lore*. Even more difficult was focusing on the words coming from Mrs. Peabody's bulbous mouth (she was a toad shifter).

The short, squat woman droned on and on about the elegance of the shifter race and how it all began. It was actually fairly interesting subject matter, but her voice made it boring.

"When animals shared their bond with certain select humans, and humans did so with animals..." Toad Lady prattled on.

Ava's head jerked up. *Wait, did she seriously just say that the shifter race began because people got it on with animals? That can't be right...* Ava started thumbing backward through the pages of her textbook to figure out what she had missed. She clearly wasn't paying proper attention.

Here we go, okay. That's reassuring. Apparently it all stems back from sorcery. There were magical people, and magical animals, and at one point, they shared their magic with each other. Phew.

"It's truly a great privilege..." Mrs. Peabody was saying.

Ava certainly didn't feel very privileged at the moment. Coming to this school was already a mistake she sorely regretted. Then she caught herself. If she had never come to the academy, she wouldn't have met her friends. She should be happy and not sitting there feeling sorry for herself. Plus, she never would have met Tarun....

Not that that mattered now.

Although, despite the horrible things she said to him, he still stood up for her to Elaine. Maybe she should make things right with him. Apologize. She could just tell him she was briefly possessed by the devil or something. Or claim temporary insanity. Yeah, that would work.

That boy was a puzzle she couldn't fit together properly. He was clearly one of the popular guys in the school, yet he chose to talk to her. The tabby cat. And not just talk to her, but kiss her! And he did all this on top of ignoring Elaine, one of the— admittedly—prettiest girls at the school. But she had yet to find out why. Tarun could literally have his pick of anyone he wanted at the school—probably even the older girls. So what did he want with her?

As the teacher continued on about the first shifter lineage, Ava decided to keep herself awake by writing her letter to her mother. Finally. At least maybe then she could get some sort of confirmation. Confirmation she badly needed.

With her heavy hair shadowing her face, she

leaned forward as discreetly as possible, hoping the teacher would just think she was taking notes, and she began to scrawl.

Hey Mom,

How are you? How is Buster? Are you both missing me terribly? I'm doing great here. The academy is everything I hoped it would be, and everyone here is super nice to me. Having the best time.

Anyway, I found something in the school library that got me curious. I'm sure you'd understand. I saw an old picture of Dad here in one of the yearbooks, and I was wondering if you knew he went to the school, too? Also, what kind of shifter was he? It's kind of important. I really need to know as soon as possible because I think it might help me with some of my classes. Please write back as soon as you can.

I love you,

Ava

PS: I'm sorry, I know you really don't like talking about Dad. Just this once. Please?

Hopefully that would do the trick. She tried to butter her up at the beginning as much as possible so that maybe she'd be more willing to spill the beans to her. If Lucy thought everything was splendid, maybe she'd be so excited for her she'd happily offer up the information.

Ava closed the book over her letter. She'd mail it after class.

"There was a Blessing—hundreds of them—walking the earth freely back then. The purest creatures that knew no harm, but they were wild. None could ride them."

What was she on about now? A blessing of some kind?

"Unfortunately, these unicorns were later slaughtered..."

Unicorns! Ava sat up straighter in her seat. Mrs. Peabody had meant a Blessing of Unicorns. Her attention now piqued.

"...for many reasons," the toad went on. "Some wanted their blood because legends said drinking it would make one immortal. Others wanted to harvest their horns for a similar reason."

Ava shifted forward in her seat.

"The unicorn horn had the magical ability to heal anyone instantly. One touch of the horn could cure anything. Even death, if the touch came soon enough."

Holy smokes! Unicorn horns are that powerful and the school is using the dust to power the ship? That is absolutely blasphemous.

"When it was discovered that just shaving dust

from the unicorn's horn, or extracting a little of the blood, could get the same effect, they were hunted and killed off rapidly."

The teacher then cleared her throat and wrote the word "Origin" on the chalkboard in big letters. Then she went on. "Seeing as they were nearly gone, they wanted to keep their race alive, but also continue to help people and other animals. Knowing extinction was not far off, they gave to a group of magical humans the ability to become one with the Blessing. To change into their own breed."

"Unicorn shifters," Ava whispered.

"And that filtered down to other shifters we have today." A puff of chalk dust kicked up as the teacher tossed the chalk down, hitting the eraser. "And there you have it, children. To the best of our knowledge, unicorns were responsible for creating the original shifter race. Had they not bestowed their magic upon humans so long ago, the magical human race, or mages as so many now know them, would never have existed. And once the mages had that kind of magic, they were able to create all kinds of other shifters. And... Voilà!" She held out her pudgy little hands, indicating to the room full of students.

"And that, dear students, is where your school gets its name. Animage is the name for a mage who can transform into an animal. A magical animal." She looked around, peeking over her little round spectacles. "Any questions?"

Probably thirty hands shot up in the air. Yes, they had questions.

One of those hands belonged to Ava, and Ava focused all her attention on the little toad lady, willing her to call on her. It worked.

"Yes, you in the back. What was your name again?"

Ava told her her name and then proceeded. "According to what you're saying, all shifters are actually mages? So that means we all have some sort of magical power?"

Mrs. Peabody bobbed her head from side to side. "Well, yes and no. We all indeed have magic to an extent. We wouldn't be able to shift if we didn't. But some are definitely blessed with more than others. For instance, your headmistress. She can utilize quite a bit of it. There's another one of you here... Oh, where are you, Azar?" She scanned the room. "Oh, there you are. Please, stand up."

Ava heard a shocked squeal come from someone about five rows in front of her. Then, a very tiny, black-haired girl stood up. The phoenix! So that was her name—Azar.

"Azar here is a phoenix shifter, and they have

tremendous magical powers. So obviously, she has more magic than the rest of you."

Azar shook uncontrollably. Ava pitied her. This girl clearly did not like being the center of attention, and attention seemed to be all she got.

"That's another reason plain shifters, such as house pets or other domesticated animals with no impressive abilities"—Ava cringed—"tend to seek out vampires or werewolves and the like."

What? Some people actually seek those monsters out on purpose? That seemed absurd to Ava. But many others around her, including Winta and JiSoo, were murmuring their agreement and nodding their heads. So apparently that was common knowledge.

"And every shifter's magic is different. Sometimes it doesn't come from the animal they shift into, like the griffin or the phoenix." She gestured for Azar to sit down, and Azar was more than happy to oblige. "Sometimes it comes from the bloodline of the mage. In those instances, you could end up with something like a fox shifter who can cast spells or control the weather."

A few more hands went up, but Mrs. Peabody ignored them. "We have to finish up here, but I want to make one more point about the unicorns."

All the raised hands went down.

"When the unicorns created the mages, and then mixed with them, making unicorn shifters, their bloodline didn't remain entirely pure. Drinking the blood of the unicorn shifter doesn't give one immortality the way it did if one drank the blood of a pure unicorn. Instead, it does give prolonged life, and also extended healing abilities. With access to enough of it, the drinker could live for hundreds and hundreds, if not thousands, of years."

Wow...

Ava exhaled with the rest of the class. Mrs. Peabody definitely had their rapt attention now after practically boring them to death for weeks. Ava wondered to herself if she would ever have the chance to meet one of these exquisite creatures. Were they really extinct? Heck, even meeting the shifter version would be cool, too.

"Sadly, these exquisite creatures are now completely extinct."

Meh.

"The last pure unicorn perished in the early 1100s. After that, unicorn shifters thrived for some time, but, along with shifting, they were also immortal. And they could heal with the touch of the horn, as you already know, but the shavings and the powder were used for various purposes." Mrs. Peabody curled her lip in distaste. "Purposes that were horrifically abused. Therefore, resulting in their eventual extinction."

Another detail Ava desperately wanted to know more about. She made a mental note to research more about this dust after mailing her letter.

Another hand shot up. It was Gregory the panda this time. The teacher checked her watch and then nodded, beckoning for the student to hurry.

"Ma'am, if unicorns are immortal, then how are they extinct? What's their weakness?"

Well, that was a darn good question. Why hadn't Ava thought of that?

Mrs. Peabody stretched her pudgy little arms as wide as they could go. "Nature always maintains balance. There is a weakness for every creature. For unicorns, it's the horn. Once the horn is completely severed, it dies. But there were rumors that if even a little part of the horn was left behind, the creature could come back to life. So it is suspected there is unicorn dust very well hidden in certain locations around the world. It is rumored there are entire secret sects devoted to resurrecting the unicorn race."

Gregory wasn't satisfied. "So every unicorn that died was a result of human invasion?"

"Humans, vampires, werewolves, other shifters

of all kinds. You name it. Everyone wanted a piece of these magical creatures. They were hunted, held captive, and butchered until there were none left. Up until maybe ten years ago, there were still a few of them. Maybe two or three, but they have since been killed off as well."

Mrs. Peabody wiped her sweaty brows with a handkerchief she pulled from her breast pocket. "It's a sad tale to tell, and I don't much enjoy it. Even when I was a girl, unicorns were still worshiped. Children adored them. Adults, too. But the poachers went too far. I even had the pleasure of teaching one when I came to the academy. But it's all over now. Does that answer your question, Gregory?"

"It does, Ma'am." Gregory looked so shocked he might cry.

Just then, the bell rang.

"Perfect timing. See you next week, class!"

As Ava leaned down to put her book back into her backpack, JiSoo leaned over Winta to say to her, "You look like hell."

Ava just looked up and glared. "Thank you for that, JiSoo. It's nice to know I look like I feel."

Winta intervened. "I think, what she means to say, is that you look very upset about something."

Ava shook her hair away from her face. "That was just a lot, you know? I feel so bad for those poor unicorns. But it also gave me an idea."

"You think your father might have been a mage?" Winta asked, reading her mind.

"So you caught on to that, too?" Ava smiled at her friend, so glad they were always on the same page.

"It definitely makes the most sense. Are you wanting to head to the library today?"

"You bet." Ava turned to look at JiSoo again. "JiSoo? Do you want to join us? Hey! Earth to JiSoo!"

JiSoo was staring, practically googly eyed, at one of the bunny shifters a little way ahead. He was chatting with his other friends as they headed out of the room. But before he got to the door, he turned back and flashed JiSoo a smile.

JiSoo's face immediately turned bright red.

"You didn't tell me you had a crush! Who is he?" Ava smiled eagerly.

JiSoo groaned and slumped her thin shoulders. "He's not my crush. He's just a boy..."

"Oh, really now?" Winta taunted her. "Because he was just staring at you like you have all the answers to life."

JiSoo elbowed her. "That's not true."

"Oh, yes, it is," Ava agreed. "I think we should

go get him right now and ask him." Ava stood up from her seat.

"Okay, okay, fine!" JiSoo jumped up as well, smiling ruefully. "Maybe I think he's nice and kind of cute."

"And?" Winta was standing now as well.

JiSoo became suddenly fascinated with her plastic bubble-tea key chain dangling from her backpack strap. "And there was this one time... shortly before I met you..."

Ava whirled around because she'd been about to walk out of the room. "Omigod! What? What happened? You better tell us *everything!*"

JiSoo looked off to the right and pressed her tongue to the inside of her cheek. "Let's just say I hope never to swallow that much of someone else's saliva ever again."

"Ewww!" Ava and Winta exclaimed together.

Ava made gagging noises, holding her belly and bending forward.

"It wasn't that bad," JiSoo defended. "He might improve. And besides, he's still pretty cute."

Laughing jovially, the three friends exited the classroom together and headed down the hallway. Land shifters poured out of classes on the right, reuniting with the water shifters who were entering the big double doors at the end of the hall from the courtyard. It sounded as if everyone was shouting the building down. Ava just kept her eyes on her friends.

With every new experience that came to her at Animage, she was forever grateful to have her unique friends by her side. Especially because now she would need their help and support when she went on her quest to learn more about unicorns, mages, and if her father had magic.

22

Tarun had one job: patrol the grounds. And he'd be damned if he spent the entire time thinking about a girl who didn't care if he lived or died. He was certain she was relieved not to see him in any of her classes today.

He told himself he was fine with it. She was just one girl after all, so what did it matter if she'd rejected him? Okay, not just rejected—practically spat on him?

He patrolled the perimeter again, needlessly; there was no one or thing nearby. Levine just liked to be certain that no one crossed it without her authorization. Although the only way to come in was via the ocean, which was nearby the school. And it was the only way to access the city above.

It was quite the honor, actually. He and several other stronger shifters were selected to miss a full day of classes to patrol the grounds, and it was his day. And he was the only first-year in the bunch. Great timing too; he wasn't sure he could face her after what she did.

There were six of them, each in their animal form, a midnight black wolf, a bear—she stood over eight feet tall, intimidating with her snarling jaws, and long sharp claws—who reclined under a tree, dozing lightly. Then there was a kangaroo—she appeared defenseless at first glance, but Tarun knew she could tear someone to pieces if provoked, and a golden brown lion patrolling beside him. Above his head flew a red dragon—he completed the pack of six.

He'd tried to sleep, to eat the meat they'd been given an hour ago, but it was impossible. Lie all he wanted to himself, he missed her, and most importantly, he was worried sick about her.

He knew firsthand what those birds of prey were capable of, and if he hadn't been there to dispel it, Elaine may have caused more damage to Ava's name. He also knew how vindictive the entire student body as a whole could be. Shifters or not, they were still teenagers. Not unlike the eagle that started it, most of those teenage shifters couldn't wait for someone to gang up on. Bullies. Ava's porcelain face floated to his mind again, for the third time in a span of maybe a few minutes. Her eyes—always sad, always lonely—called to him.

All he wanted was to please her, to keep her smiling. If he could, he'd single-handedly break down all the segregation in the school, make them see that everyone was the same, that no one got to choose what they would be, but that was not in his power. What he *could* do, however, was get back to her as soon as his shift was finished.

Also, he didn't believe a single thing Elaine said about her. He would confirm everything with Ava and Winta himself.

Soon.

He resumed patrolling, his mind made up to talk to her.

23

"When?"

"At night."

"Ava, do you really wish to go home that bad?" Winta stood akimbo.

"I think it's perfect timing," JiSoo defended Ava.

"Thanks, JiSoo. Look, Winta, it's the best time," Ava wheedled.

"No, you look at me, you are not listening." Winta's accent got extra thick when she was trying to make a point. "I told you there was a way we could access those records. Daytime, no problem...you want to repeat the same mistake?"

"Of course not. That's not the point." Ava folded her arms.

Winta threw her hands up. "Then what is, Ava? Because, this is not working."

They were sitting huddled together in the dining hall, whispering hotly. It was dinnertime, and Ava hadn't seen a glimpse of Tarun. It was driving her insane, as was the letter to her mother burning a hole in her purse.

"Okay, I'm sorry, I just wanted to get on with it, that's all."

Winta, always the one with the sense of reason, placed a calming hand on her shoulder. The three of them had rushed through their food, and their plates sat empty between them.

"All right, we'll go after the first class...aaaaand I've lost you... What are y—oh." She followed Ava's gaze to where Tarun was greeting his friends with slaps on the back. Ava didn't recognize them; they looked older. Was that a fourth-year kangaroo making eyes at him??? His deep baritone laughter floated to her ears.

That was where he belonged: in the crowds with the elite, just like him.

"Ava?"

"I don't think she knows we're here," JiSoo said, but she was also looking at Tarun. Who wouldn't? He was easily the alpha male in the room, even among those older predators.

"Ava? Earth to Ava," Winta snapped her fingers in front of her face, and Ava returned to her senses.

JiSoo reached over to her with a white napkin, "I'm just gonna wipe that drool."

Ava snorted—a very unladylike sound—and swatted JiSoo's hands away. "It's not that bad." But she stylishly checked to see if there was a line of saliva running down her mouth.

"So, when are you gonna talk to him?" JiSoo pressed.

"Soon as I get the chance. He's still busy for now."

"What if he comes over here?"

"No!" She looked panicked for a second. "He wouldn't dare."

"Oh, but I think he already is," Winta pointed out as quietly as she could.

As they watched, Tarun sauntered away from his group, followed closely by James who'd probably been waiting for the opportunity to see Winta.

Ava gulped the water in her glass at one go, then averted her eyes from him, scared she would make a fool out of herself if she stared hungrily at him, just the way she craved to.

Out of the corner of her eyes, Ava saw Elaine glaring at Tarun's back. She quelled the urge to laugh out loud.

Wait, she was jumping to conclusions; for all

she knew, he was coming to give her a piece of his mind.

"Hey Winta, JiSoo." He flashed the girls another one of his disarming smiles.

Ava pretended not to hear, even when her friends fell over themselves to make space for him.

"Ava?" he greeted her, too.

Grudgingly, she dragged her eyes up to meet his. She was prepared for the jolt this time and kept her eyes on him. But lord, did he have to be soooo striking? He practically smoldered. Just looking at him turned her insides to mush.

"Oh, hi, didn't see you there." *So obviously lying.*

His eyebrow slid up, amused. "Doesn't matter, I see you."

She forced herself to remain stoic, even when everything in her screamed to be let go, to gush like all the other girls were doing, but she stilled against it.

Their eyes held across the table. Everything seemed to fade away. The noise in the dining hall receded. The clatter of spoons and forks against plates fell silent. All that remained—to Ava, at least—was Tarun, in that moment.

She caved. "I'm sorry," Ava mouthed...or did she say it out loud? She wasn't sure.

"I understand." He held her gaze.

Did he really, though?

There were no more words, none were enough to describe how she felt in that moment, that second.

Then the bell went off, interrupting whatever he was about to say.

About fifty chairs scraped back at once, pulling Ava back to the present. Beside her, James was trying his best to make Winta laugh; he'd inserted chopsticks in his mouth—they stuck out like fangs —and he wiggled his thick eyebrows at her. Probably trying to be a walrus.

Winta chuckled and scraped her chair back, too. Tarun held out his hand for Ava. James walked between JiSoo and Winta, smiling widely.

The guys accompanied the girls to their dormitory. Ava couldn't believe she and Tarun had just resolved everything so easily. Everything just felt perfectly relaxed and comfortable now. How was that even possible?

"I'll see you tomorrow at lunch," he said to her as they approached her room. JiSoo had already disappeared inside, and Winta had walked off with James.

"What makes you think I want to see you?" she fired back playfully. *Uh oh. Was that too harsh?*

"I want to, shouldn't that be enough?" He grinned with the side of his mouth.

Okay, she hadn't screwed things up again. Ava suddenly felt tired of the games and nodded, "I can't wait to see you, too."

He broke into the widest smile she had seen on him yet, exposing his perfect white teeth.

"Okay, Ava, good night." He backed away slowly, still looking at her.

She stood at the door, watching until he turned and went out of sight. A little sigh escaped her before she went inside her room to gush to JiSoo.

The day may have begun badly, but it sure ended on a pleasant note.

Elaine, however, still sulking in the dining hall, was fuming. Her day was ruined, destroyed! She'd figured Tarun would hear all the rumors and run back to her screaming. Instead, she'd succeeded in driving them together.

The knife in her heart twisted viciously. No, there was no way that little brat was going to get all this, and she knew just what to do. Obviously Ava was beginning to feel like the queen, and what did a queen need?

A befitting crown.

Elaine was more than ready to gift her one.

All she had to do was wait for daylight.

She slunk to her room, avoiding Deacon who leered at her. He was persistent, and though she wanted to use him to get back at Tarun, she didn't want to deal with him right now. Boys tended to ruin things. If she was going to do this, she'd trust only one person to execute it perfectly: herself.

24

The girls had been unfaltering in their decision not to break into the library one more time. JiSoo had to be convinced further by Winta before she caved.

That afternoon, after classes, they took a detour to the mailing room. Considering the ancient ways of the school, the mailing room was the most sophisticated.

Bunny shifters of all shapes and sizes worked there in their animal forms. Some were adults employed by the academy, others were students trying to earn extra credits. She even saw the kid who transformed on the first day at the security area. He seemed to have adjusted well—didn't appear lost in the midst of others like him.

The room was enormous, a busy cavern that never slept.

"Winta, does your dad have a place like this, too?" Ava asked as she looked all around her.

Winta laughed. "Be serious, Girl, letters disappeared with the email era. Animage is probably the only place around that still has an operation like this."

JiSoo, who was yet to be caught up on Winta's wealthy family, looked blank. Ava filled her in as they walked straight to the mailing counter. Several students had beat them to it, and so the line was fairly long.

They settled in to wait Ava's turn. She took the time to survey her surroundings more. Next to the wall, five large printers were lined up, manned by five bunnies per machine. She wondered how they didn't get swallowed by the ginormous printers.

She giggled and pointed them out to her friends. Five bunnies climbed atop each other's heads, ears flapping. They formed a little pyramid, and the top one tethered and steadied itself, then continued to retrieve papers like it was nothing.

"They're so cute..." JiSoo melted to mush beside her.

"Can you recognize any from our year?"

"Sure, he's waving at me right now," JiSoo answered. "See?" She pointed.

"How can you tell?" Winta squinted at the "waving" bunny. "Wait, is he your crush?"

JiSoo blushed furiously and prettily. "No, I told you, I don't like him like that..."

"But he likes you, oh—he's coming over...look away!"

The girls hustled to appear lost in conversation. The little bunny transformed into a handsome Asian boy as he made his way to them. JiSoo, unfortunately, collided with the boy as he finished his shift, causing a mini avalanche as the boy knocked down three more in the line.

JiSoo opened her mouth and eyes in horror, temporarily forgetting where they stood....

It was bad.

Her right eye popped out first, the left following shortly after. The boy, the reason for the avalanche, noticed the trouble and quickly morphed back to bunny form and scurried away.

Everyone in line, except her friends, screamed, running off in different directions at once upon seeing JiSoo's black empty sockets. Thankfully, no one stepped on the eyeballs that had rolled under their feet.

Winta and Ava hustled to find them before they disappeared behind the massive counter.

"Here, JiSoo, sorry." Winta handed one back to her.

Ava wordlessly gave her the other.

JiSoo lifted her eyebrows and pushed one in, then the other. Ava cringed—that was *so* unsanitary! By the time she was through, only the attendants, who seemed to have seen it all, remained. Every other shifter had left the line and fled.

"Are you okay?" Ava asked her friend.

"I'm fine, I'm fine, okay?" Even though she looked like she was trying not to cry. "Just mail the letter, and let's get out of here."

Ava knew JiSoo was hurting by the way her back stiffened and her chin wobbled. She clearly struggled so hard to keep up the façade of confidence.

She pushed the letter to the hands of the waiting attendant—a bunny shifter in his human form. He took it and filed it under a sign that read: 'Miami Delivery.'

"I'm done," she announced, "That wasn't as hard as I thought. I have to admit, I'm grateful you got rid of that line for me." She tried to lift JiSoo's spirits a little. "For some reason, I pictured talking pigeons and owls."

That wrangled a smile from her sullen roommate at least, and they emerged from the mailing room together and headed outside. Ava had converted Winta and JiSoo to loving the outdoors as much as she did.

"That was classic, JiSoo." Winta couldn't hold in her laughter any longer. Immediately after stepping outside, and she was safely out of JiSoo's reach, she doubled over and laughed heartily, snorting adorably at the end of each laugh.

Her laughter was infectious, and Ava soon joined in, mimicking the utter horror in the other shifters' faces when JiSoo's eye fell at their feet. Soon, JiSoo's initial annoyance changed to mild amusement as she watched her friends.

"Great, you guys know you're being mean, right?" But she was now grinning foolishly, the annoyance having evaporated completely, leaving her smiling sheepishly.

"That had to be the biggest kerfuffle I've seen since I came to this school." Winta stood back upright, and they started walking down the pathway to the tree they had claimed as their own. Usually they sat underneath until it was time for the next class.

On getting to the tree, they heard the squeals first.

"What the heck? No one else likes to sit there, much less talk to us," Ava speculated. They walked a bit slower until they could see.

Behind the tree, where the girls claimed as their spot, Elaine and her gang were crowded there.

Elaine spotted them first, and she cornered Ava. "Can we talk?" She eyed Ava's friends. "Privately."

Ava's hackles rose—or they would have if she were in her cat form—instantly alert. Quickly she scanned the area to see if someone was about to jump on her,

"Relax. If I wanted to harm you, you'd be seriously wounded by now."

She had a point. Ava nodded. What could she do in a public place anyway...? She followed Elaine away from both of their groups of friends.

"Okay, I'm just gonna go ahead and say it." Elaine folded her arms. "I'm sorry for the way things turned out between us. I was blinded by jealousy. You had everything I wanted, and you didn't even know it. You spent all your time hiding in the shadows, when you could easily shine. I was jealous when Tarun saw that in you, too, so I wanted to break you."

Ava stood there dumbfounded. Did Elaine really just not only apologize to her, but actually admit her own faults? This was the best day ever! "Elaine, if you're trying to apologize, then I accept it. I never liked the fights—"

"Me either. I don't know what got into me. I'm so sorry."

"Really?"

"Yeah, I want us to start over...become friends, the way we should have been when you came to the room." The eagle looked the cat directly in the eyes as she spoke. She looked so sincere. "I resented you then, but now all I want is to be your friend. Ava, do you think that's possible? Can we start over?"

Ava was stunned for a few seconds before she recovered her tongue enough to speak. There she was, imagining all the things that could go wrong before the end of the semester if Elaine continued to see her as the enemy, and now it was suddenly a non-issue. But, still, there was a little voice in her head telling her not to take this apology at face value. "I want to talk to my friends first."

Elaine's face pinched. "Okay, but we accept one friend at a time." The way "friend" dripped from her lips sent shivers of pleasure down Ava's spine. She was ready, more than ready, to stop being bullied and finally be accepted by the popular clique in school. Besides, if they accepted her, then people wouldn't mock her and Tarun when they were together.

With those thoughts on her mind, she stepped away from Elaine and ran back to Winta and JiSoo who had walked a fair distance away, but still stood to watch.

"Did you see that?!" Ava squealed excitedly when she got closer to them.

They wore matching expressions of confusion stamped on their faces.

"Elaine apologized! She wants to be my friend, can you imagine?!"

Winta and JiSoo exchanged looks. Then Winta said, "I *can't* imagine, no. So what was your answer?"

"I told her I wanted to run it by you guys first."

Winta's shoulders relaxed.

"Tell me, you don't buy any of that crap, do you, Ava?" JiSoo added.

"What crap? You should have seen her, heard her, she sounded sincere!" She had expected her friends to be happy for her, so why were they being so negative?

"Ava, she's setting you up for something, can't you feel it?" JiSoo squeezed her hands into fists.

"She's definitely using you. I thought you'd be smart enough to realize that. C'mon Ava, tell me you're not considering her offer!" Winta chided.

"Excuse me?" Ava flared her nostrils. How dare Winta talk to her like she was dumb! Now she could see what they were doing. "You're just jealous she doesn't want *you*."

Her friends reared back—a slap may have hurt less. Ava almost regretted her words—almost.

JiSoo's chin went up. "Fine. Do what you like, but don't forget we warned you. Let's go, Winta. Clearly Ava has new friends now." Coldly, JiSoo turned away, obviously expecting Winta to do the same.

Winta looked directly into Ava's eyes, silently pleading with her. "This is a mistake, Ava. And I know you feel it, too." Then she turned and followed JiSoo away.

Ava's mind was made up. Her friends didn't want good things to come her way, but they would change their minds soon enough.

Didn't they see this was an opportunity for all of them? That Elaine had finally come to her senses? Her friends were wrong. She was going to explore this, and finally gain some popularity at the school. Then they would come crawling—no, *running*—back to her.

"I'll see you later." She returned coldly to their retreating backs, and then she pirouetted to meet her newest friends.

25

Being one of the popular girls was a whirlwind of makeup, hair spray, and idle gossip.

Ava felt lost in a haze of mascara, shiny pink lip gloss, eyelash curlers, hair dryers, and a host of other beauty unnecessary products. Then there was her new wardrobe. Apparently everything she brought with her was absolute crap. Elaine loaned her a pair of sparkly black pumps and taught her how to cinch her uniform dress so it showed off more of her body. Admittedly, Ava had always wondered why the popular girls looked better in their uniforms. She'd figured they were just more blessed in the curve department, but now her uniform held to every curve of her body, highlighting every crevice that was there and even what wasn't.

She twirled in front of the mirror, unbelieving. She didn't know the girl looking back at her. Elaine had worked her magic, and now Ava's eyes appeared big and smoky, her fake lashes accentuated her look, and her bright pink lips made her look more like a doll than a sixteen-year-old girl. They'd even applied acrylic glittering nails, and added highlights to her hair.

"You like?" Elaine queried.

Like? Ava felt like she was about to die of happiness. Sure, she might not have chosen that much makeup for herself, and she thought the shoes kind of made her look like a "lady of the night,"—as her mom would say—but for the first time, as she looked at herself, she felt...sexy. And she no longer felt self-conscious about her dingy brown hair. It was bright and pretty and full of life, thanks to the highlights and the curling iron.

"I love it all. Thank you. Thank you so much!" Ava gushed, rushing over to throw her arms around Elaine. She heard one of the others cough uncomfortably, but decided maybe she was wrong. After all, it was hard to tell with the dangling earrings making clinking noises in her eardrums. It felt like they were going to mar her hearing permanently.

"I'm glad." Elaine clapped. "You're perfect."

"I am?" Ava whispered, then turned to look at herself in the mirror again. "I am!"

"Good, now let's get to class!" Lois chimed in, flipping her platinum ponytail.

Ava couldn't wait for Tarun to see her and fall head over heels in love. But she also wondered if the change was too abrupt and maybe she'd overdone it. "You're sure this isn't too much, right?"

"You look absolutely fabulous," Elaine crooned. "Right, girls?"

There was a chorus of, "Yes... Of course..." From the others, although Ava was fairly certain she heard Lorraine stifle a laugh.

Together, they all lifted their individual purses, each competing in size and designer brand name. Ava reached for her simple black shoulder bag, which, until that morning, she had thought was perfect for her.

"Oh no, you can't take *that*." Elaine hopped over to her closet again and retrieved a little gold clutch from her stash. "Here you go. But I'll be wanting this back after you get your own."

Reluctantly, Ava transferred some of her stuff to the clutch, even though it wasn't as spacious. She was forced to put the rest in her backpack.

Elaine looked her over one more time and decided it was time to go.

When Ava stepped out into the hallway for the first time with the popular girls, she felt on top of the world.

26

Winta and JiSoo had wasted no time. Immediately after Ava's decision to ditch them, they had run straight to Tarun to inform him of Ava's temporary madness, as JiSoo termed it.

Tarun's lips turned down. "Are you sure those were her exact words?"

JiSoo nodded emphatically. "She was out of her mind! You should've seen her! We couldn't talk sense into her, even a little. I even tried to convince her when she stopped back in our room to grab a few things, but she snubbed me. *Me!*" JiSoo paced back and forth dramatically, gesturing with her hands as if she were performing in a Shakespearean play. She was so riled up that Tarun could barely decipher her Korean accent.

Scratching his upper lip, Tarun got moving down the hall again. He had been on his way to evening training, but had stopped to give Winta and JiSoo his full attention when they came bounding at him out of nowhere, freaking out about Ava's behavior. And now he could understand why. "That doesn't sound like Ava at all. Don't worry, I'll talk to her if I can get her alone."

James, trailing along behind Tarun, waved eagerly at Winta.

JiSoo shot him a glare, then turned back to Tarun and said, "We understand, but that's not the point. It's bad enough that she's being a total jerk, but we all know someone like Elaine is not just going to forgive Ava easily. Ava is about to get seriously hurt. I just know it."

Tarun stopped walking again. The little pug shifter was completely right. He tousled his white hair and groaned. "We'll see where it goes. But like I said, don't worry. I'll talk to her."

"Yeah, don't worry, Winta," James said, removing a nonexistent flake from Winta's shoulder.

Winta just rolled her eyes.

When Tarun saw Ava with the flock for the first time the next morning, he nearly stumbled on his own two feet. She looked gorgeous, that was certain, but also extremely overdone and not at all like herself. However, one thing could be said: Elaine had brought out something in Ava that she'd been lacking previously.

Confidence.

And that confidence was extremely becoming. Unfortunately, she'd also strolled past him like he wasn't there. And he would be blind not to notice pretty much every guy at the school, and even a few girls, looking her over. Some even whistled, and he wanted to beat them up. All these jerks who had been so mean to her just days before shouldn't be allowed to gawk now.

He knew he had to find a solution. He'd initially thought it would be easy to talk sense into her, but now that he saw her with her nose in the air like that, he knew it would be harder than he expected. In some ways, perhaps it would be better for him to just back off and let her make her own mistakes. She'd learn from them, for sure.

He'd just made it to his morning class. All the first-years were in this one together. Winta and JiSoo sat together in the back, glaring at Ava. Tarun sat only a few seats away from them, next to James. Ava followed Elaine and the others to the other side of the room, joining them toward the front alongside Deacon and the other predators.

Suddenly, a voice very close to his ear startled him. "Elaine told me to give this to you." It was Colin, and he passed a note to him before returning to his seat near Ava and the other birds of prey.

Tarun unfolded the note and looked it over. Elaine's signature perfume wafted to his nostrils.

Tarun,

I'm sorry about everything. You were right, I was blinded by jealousy. Let me make it up to you.

E

"What's it say?" James squinted over his shoulder.

Tarun handed him the note.

"Geez. What's gotten into her?" James said after reading it.

"No idea," Tarun muttered.

"Sounds like she actually feels bad."

"Ava's friends think Elaine is using her."

"I guess, but she seems pretty harmless now. You could hear her out at least..." James shrugged one shoulder.

Tarun shrugged right back. "Anyway, I guess I can talk to her after class. Maybe I can talk to Ava, too."

. . .

Class went by way too slowly for Tarun's liking, but after the instructor dismissed them, he waited for Winta and JiSoo to leave the room before he approached any of the predators. Luckily, Winta and JiSoo were on the side closest to the door, so they exited way before. Instead of leaving with them, he waved them along and waited with James until Elaine came closer to them.

But before he had a chance to say anything to Elaine, Deacon walked up to them. "Are you trying to bang that African elephant?" he asked James with a sneer.

Out of the corner of his eye, Tarun could see Elaine disappearing out the door with Ava right next to her.

Crap.

"What?" James looked taken aback. "It's nothing. She's just really nice, and funny...and smart..."

"And huge," one of Deacon's bear friends quipped by his side.

"And ugly," another said.

"And filthy." They were on a roll.

"I heard she trashed her room once, just trying to roll over in her sleep..."

"Imagine her taking a dump... Whoa!"

"Enough!" James smacked his fist on the little

fold-out desk next to him. Luckily, the teacher was no longer in the room to see his outburst.

James's face was red, his breathing erratic. But still, he defended her. "She is more human and definitely more beautiful than any of you!"

None of them had the grace to look ashamed at all. Rather, one of the bear shifters beside Deacon snorted, "A hummingbird and an elephant... Damn! You better hope she never shifts by accident while you guys are getting in on. She'll crush you to death before she even realizes what happened." And then they all burst out laughing.

That was it. Tarun pressed back, ready to knock someone's teeth out. He couldn't let James take this, and he didn't like the horrible things they were saying about his new friends. Winta was awesome. And besides, Tarun could handle getting beaten up, but James couldn't. Sure, Tarun might get kicked out of the academy, but he highly doubted it because he held a pretty prestigious position—ya know, white tiger and all....

Unfortunately, he wasn't fast enough. James tried to take the first swing already. Tarun didn't even know if James had been aiming for Deacon, or one of the others, but he missed completely and toppled forward. That didn't stop him though. In seconds, James was back up on his feet, swinging violently again. Tarun shot forward and held him back before he got James teeth knocked out.

"Let me go!" James flailed. "These assholes have to learn not to talk about people that way!"

Instead, Tarun pressed him down into the closest seat and stood over him. Moving his hands to James's shoulders, he stared him in the eyes. "Forget it, James. They're not worth the trouble."

"So cute," Colin chuckled. "Couple of fags."

Tarun pressed his lips together and just kept staring at James. It was clear they both had the same thought: *Kill.*

Then, taking a deep breath, Tarun remembered what was more important. Attending this school was a huge deal, even for him. There was no guarantee he would get to stay if he hurt another student badly enough. Even if it was justified. His entire future would be down the toilet just like that.

James seemed to come to the same conclusion right when he did because his shoulders softened.

Tarun stepped back and extended his hand to James, helping him up.

"Let's get out of here," Tarun suggested. "These guys aren't worth our time."

Sitting in the next period, waiting for the bell to ring, Ava found herself between the twins. Lois, Breanna, and Lorraine sat to her right. Elaine stood in front of them, shifting her hips back and forth.

"It's appalling!" Elaine complained.

"I know, it's like she's blind," Lorraine agreed.

"Do you think she got dressed in the dark this morning?" Daniella's large lips flattened in disgust.

The girls were talking about a nearby wolf shifter.

Frankly, Ava didn't understand what the problem was. They had to wear uniforms anyway, so what didn't they like? Aside from the uniform dress, the girl was wearing knee-high boots and a black sweater. Maybe it was her hair? She was wearing it in kind of a messy bun... Maybe messy buns weren't in style anymore?

Ava, unlike her new friends, didn't care at all about looks or shoes or purses or piles and piles of makeup. Ava actually thought the wolf girl was beautiful, and she said as much.

The twins gasped in horror at Ava's revelation, then all the girls started talking at once.

Finally, Elaine raised her perfectly manicured hand and pressed the side of her hot pink finger-nail to her lips and shushed them. "Ava is right."

Once again, the girls gasped collectively. But

Lorraine didn't buy it and opened her mouth to object.

But Elaine cut her off. "She does have a certain aura about her, right, Ava?"

Ava nodded enthusiastically. Life was so much better without enemies. Just look at her and Elaine now. After everything they'd been through, Elaine now defended her against the rumors and even against her own flock.

The only dent in her new shining armor was that Tarun had pulled away from her completely, it seemed. Maybe it was because now Elaine was stuck to her like glue at all times, and he didn't want to go near her. It made sense. Ava knew how much Tarun despised Elaine's clinginess. She would have to have a talk with him the first chance she got. Explain everything. He'd understand.

Until then, Ava had to focus on changing the way she walked, talked, just carried herself overall.

And so far, there were already several new boys trying to get her attention. It felt good...she had to admit.

Ava thought back to the previous class. Tarun had looked gorgeous, as always. And she noticed James and Winta sneaking looks at each other. She smiled at the thought. She was going to have to tease Winta about that—

Her breath caught in her throat. That's right.

Winta was avoiding her now, as was JiSoo. At breakfast, they wouldn't even look at her and they'd sat far away. And the night before, Elaine had insisted she sleep in her room with her—ironic because they used to be roommates—but that also meant she hadn't even seen JiSoo.

"Mr. Meadowlark is here!" Lois announced next to her. They all got quiet. Ava readjusted in her seat.

The man approached the podium ahead of them via a rounded set of stairs. Like Sir Waters, he walked with a cane, his cane hitting the floor with a resounding clack every step he took. Dressed in a gray suit, shoulders slumping, and his eyes distorted by big, round, coke-bottle glasses.

Ava had heard he was a dragon shifter, magnificent in his days.

But anyone looking at him now would mistake him for weak and hapless.

He cleared his throat—in the room's silence, it was like rumbling thunder. "Pop quiz!"

"Noooooo!" Everyone groaned.

After he handed out the tests, Ava scanned the questions. They were pretty easy. Mostly about the biogenetic makeup of the shifter race—a subject she had found relatively engaging.

Three minutes in, the class was interrupted.

Headmistress Levine marched in with five

attendants behind her. Her lips were thinner than usual. Mr. Meadowlark stepped back from the podium to let the headmistress speak. And speak she did! The color of her face was almost the same as the red pant suit she wore.

"Maybe we have been too lenient—lax even— this semester. That is about to change." She paused, her glare sweeping the class.

"This morning, someone stole a very important artifact from my office. I am utterly disappointed and, honestly, downright disgusted."

There was a collective gasp from almost every student in the room. Even Mr. Meadowlark looked horrified.

"The crown, that has been in my family for generations, is now missing. There will be a school-wide search until we find it. And believe me, we *will* find it. And also believe me, whoever has it should prepare to go home... After being sent to the authorities."

When the headmistress left the classroom, the whole class erupted in chatter, the test forgotten.

Ava tapped Elaine on the shoulder. Elaine was excitedly talking to Daniella, gesticulating widely. Ava ducked to avoid the flailing hand.

"What's so special about this crown?"

"You don't even know?" Elaine's lips formed a shocked, extremely red O.

Ava shook her head. No longer worrying about finishing her quiz because Mr. Meadowlark had left with the headmistress.

"But you do know the griffin family legend, right?"

"They create the glamour for the school, yes." Ava tried not to think about the moment that followed with Tarun right after he told her about that.

Elaine flipped her blonde hair. "That crown was gifted to the original griffin by a sorcerer. Sure, they learned to control their powers without it, but it's still a core part of who they are. And it's essential that it remains here at the academy for all of our protection. Whoever stole it has some serious nerve."

Ava wondered who would do such a thing and for what reason. None of them, as far as she knew, were sorcerers, so any magic that crown held would be completely lost to them.

All she could do was hope the person would return it though, then hopefully things could go right back to normal, just with one less shifter at the school.

"I guess we can go then?" Diana observed. "It looks like class is over."

They all agreed she was right and collected their belongings to leave.

"You know what this means for the thief, right?" Elaine said as they exited the classroom.

"Immediate expulsion?" Ava guessed.

"Try immediate arrest," Lois sneered.

Ava's chin jerked back. "Don't you think that's a little harsh? I mean, whoever did it is obviously just a kid, seeing as this is a school."

Elaine's head whipped back, and she stared incredulously at Ava for a few seconds.

Ava tried not to roll her eyes at all the theatrics.

"What? Harsh? You should see this crown. In fact, Levine's great-great grandmother wore it every day when she was headmistress of the school. It's everything a girl could dream about." Elaine's voice became a little breathy as she spoke about it. "I think there's a picture in the library, actually. C'mon, I'll show you. Then you tell me if you think she should be lenient."

Elaine took a sharp right turn, now headed for the library, and Ava almost crashed into her.

For a few seconds, Ava felt a hole burning in the back of her head, and just before they got to the library entrance, she swung around to see who was watching her.

Tarun.

His white hair had fallen over his dark eyes,

and he made no move to shove it out of the way. As he stared at her, she felt like he silently begged her to come back and talk to him.

Inwardly, she promised him she would. But for now, she was focused on staying on Elaine's good side. So with a small smile, she swallowed her disappointment, and continued through the halls with Elaine. Everything would be fine. She was sure of it.

"Do they have any suspects?" someone, a boy, asked from behind her. It looked like all training was officially done for the day for everyone.

Discreetly, she tilted her head to hear the answer.

"I heard it has to be a first-year—that's why Levine came to our hall."

"What gave her that impression? It could have been anybody in the academy, down to the little kids that train on the other wing of the school."

"Hey, Ava, could you hold my backpack?" Elaine shoved her heavy bag into Ava's hands without even waiting for an answer. "I just have to run a little errand. I'll join you at the library soon, okay?"

"Oh! Yeah, that's fine."

Elaine placed her hand lightly on Ava's shoulder, then bent forward slightly so they could see eye to eye. "Thank you. You're such a sweetheart. I wish we'd become friends sooner."

Ava grinned back and watched Elaine go, hips swaying admirably, like a model's. Wow. Elaine really was so nice now. Who would've thought?

"We should get going," Diane said, interrupting her musing.

"Yes, of course."

They weaved through the crowds surging from the classes, each one noisier than the next. Question flew from every angle:

"Who could've done this?"

"When does the search begin?"

"I need to clean my room!" A purple-haired fox shifter yelled and zipped past her.

She caught sight of JiSoo and Winta walking toward Indigo Dorm. She made no move to call them. In fact, she stubbornly forced her eyes away from them. There were things she had to check at the library anyway, and she still had her date with the headmistress in three days, so she had to come up with a good reason why she broke into the library without letting on that she was searching for Matthew Carrington.

Out of the hallway, they entered a dome—where most students went out to relax, meet friends, and receive mail from the bunnies zapping afoot. It had a transparent skylight—star studded, gleaming like diamonds. She never came out here —she always took the hallway detour. Popular kids and seniors made it a hangout, so she had usually avoided it.

She saw Tarun and James sitting together on one of the velour couches toward the back. He looked perfectly happy now. No hint of the disappointment she'd seen in his eyes just a few minutes ago.

Tremors ran through her body as she remembered that kiss out in the fields. She wanted a repeat. His hands on her back, in her hair...

Focus, Ava!

Finally, they came out to the massive doors...and now two attendants. Levine had strengthened the security. On the sides of the door, giant gargoyles stood guard. Had those always been there?

She shook it off, but if she blurred her eyes a bit, the gargoyles looked straight at her, their luminous ruby-red eyes glowing dangerously. Yikes. She hurried in with the girls, who stopped talking immediately when they stepped into the library.

"Come on, Ava, you gotta see the crown," Daniella whispered. Her twin nodded beside her, smacking her lips.

Ava frowned again—they appeared to be enjoying a joke she wasn't in on.

"Sure." She readjusted Elaine's backpack on her shoulder and followed them.

They passed the tall shelves: Religion, Legends, Shifter History, Human Fiction, several sections she missed.

Mr. Jerome, the librarian, had lowered his spunky glasses and peered suspiciously when he spotted Ava. She chuckled; the school attendants had a way of blowing minor cases out of proportion, and despite what anyone said, she didn't commit a huge crime that night. Levine wouldn't have just let her off like that if she had.

But not here. Everything was a soap opera it seemed.

They stopped at a shelf marked 'Griffin Legend.'

Lorraine picked out a small book, not more than twenty pages, maybe thirty. She thrust it at Ava, her beady eyes squinting at her. The others gathered.

Ava began to feel suffocated. It bothered her how they knew exactly where to find the tiny book. But she swallowed her doubts and opened it.

It began with the history of the crown, a short one. She figured there was more on it somewhere, but the next page was a full picture of the crown.

It's a ring?! She'd assumed they were referring to a real crown, or at least a tiara or something.

Instead, it was attached to the gnarled middle finger of an old woman.

"That's the first griffin shifter," Diane whispered. "The sorcerer gifted her the ring, helped her keep the school hidden. Told you she wore it all the time."

"You didn't say it was a ring." Ava stared at the old photo. A gem-studded ring. It was formed from thin tarnished gold on one layer, a burnished silver on top, joined by precious stones. Dead center, a raw diamond winked at her.

None of them bothered to apologize. Lorraine shrugged. "Of course it is."

Ava liked Lorraine the least—she went out of her way to make Ava feel idiotic. Like she was feeling now. And Elaine wasn't there to act as a buffer.

Needing an excuse to get out of there, she tapped Diane's arm, already shrugging off Elaine's heavy bag. "Please hold on to this for Elaine. I've got to check on something in another aisle for one of my assignments real quick... You guys don't need to come with me," she added when they started whispering to follow her. What were they, her bodyguards?

"Just be back when Elaine returns or she's gonna be pissed," Diane insisted.

"Thanks," Ava grumbled as she wandered off,

taking a deep calming breath. Finally, she was free and alone. She picked at the sides of her dress—it hugged her body tightly now. She'd be glad to take it off at the end of the day.

She crossed to the microfiche; it was ancient, but, most importantly, no one was using it at the moment. She went to the shelves behind it, tracing back the years. She checked newspapers, articles from the school paper, all in black and white. Nothing on Matthew Carrington.

Humming the *Friends* theme song, she stacked the pile of papers beside the machine. She slotted in the first paper—they won the centennial that year. A competition between shifter schools; she wasn't surprised Animage won.

Still, nothing on her father, not even a picture.

Patiently, she inserted another paper, pulled a creaky lever...

Nothing...wolf festival, snow dance, welcome dinner, inter-school festival, pictures and more pictures.

Nothing.

She continued, increasing her pace. When she was halfway down the pile, she saw a boy's collar rakishly turned up, smiling impishly at the camera. He stood in the center of a group of boys.

She rushed to read the attached article.

Matt Carrington had made the news that day.

And several days after that.

Her heart thudded, hardly believing what she saw, what she read, It said the boys by his side were alive because of him. Her father had healed those boys from some sort of plague when it hit the school. Dozens of shifters would've died if he hadn't curbed it.

The hand squeezing the lever grew cold, so cold. He could heal people? He was a hero? Her mother had kept this part from her...why would she do that?

Lucy still hadn't responded to Ava's letter, so Ava didn't know what to think. Page after page of Matthew Carrington. Then she froze.

The next picture displayed her father in his shifter form. She knew it was her father immediately before even looking at the name beneath.

She pressed her hand against her mouth. No, this wasn't possible. Yet she knew it was true: the unicorn on that page was her father.

Her dad was a unicorn shifter.

Now, more than ever, her desire to find him increased, but there was nothing in the records to even give her a hint if he was alive or not. But he couldn't be, right? Mrs. Peabody said unicorn shifters were completely extinct. So he had to be dead then.

Realizing how long she had taken already, she

replaced everything where she found it and rushed back to meet the flock.

Only they were already gone.

She hated to admit that she was more than just a little relieved not to have to see them. She passed Mr. Jerome on her way; he scanned her—okay, not stealing—and let her go.

Ava hightailed it to her room—her own room, not Elaine's—desperately trying to organize her thoughts. There was so much she had to do, to process, to sort—and it was all clashing rather painfully in her head.

Upon arriving in her room, she collapsed on her bed, dropping her gold clutch at the foot of her bed and her backpack on the floor. She knew she had failed Elaine by taking off and leaving Elaine's backpack with the rest of her flock after she'd specifically asked Ava to hold it, but she didn't much care at that point.

Lying on her bed, letting her mind race, it was a while before she remembered why JiSoo wasn't in the room: dinner.

Her stomach grumbled. She hadn't eaten since lunch, but she was too worked up to go down to the dining hall. She decided to tell JiSoo everything when she returned. Ava needed someone to talk to. Needed to organize her rambling thoughts.

With superhuman effort, she got up from her bed and headed to the bathroom for a quick shower before she turned in for the night.

But Ava hadn't gone two steps when her door reverberated...someone was pounding on it.

27

Winta picked at her food, pushing her potatoes around the plate. Occasionally, she released a heavy sigh.

When JiSoo couldn't take it any longer, she dropped her fork with a clang and faced her. "She left us, okay? We have to get over it. Her choice, remember?" She wiggled a finger at her. "Didn't you see how she completely blew us off at lunch? Didn't you?"

Winta sighed again; it had only been a couple of days and she missed Ava. The table felt incomplete without her. "She didn't blow us off, Elaine dragged her. Didn't you see?" she sulked, stabbing her food.

"You know that's not Elaine, right? You're about to murder the poor potatoes," James said, pointing at Winta's plate. He and Tarun opted to sit with the girls nowadays. Even without Ava, it was nicer than hanging out with feeding predators.

"Okay, how was your day?" James tried to change the subject.

Winta glared at him. "How do you think?" she fired back. She wanted to go over to that table where Elaine was laughing and talking with her friends and demand Ava back. Only it looked like Ava wasn't even with her now.

"Sorry, don't bite off my head."

She groaned, "I didn't mean it like that. Hey, do you know if they've searched our wing yet?"

"Yeah, I saw attendants on the way here, pounding on doors," James replied.

"Although why they think we would steal and then leave it in school beats me," Tarun muttered, little above a whisper.

Winta craned her neck, trying to catch a glimpse of Ava, but she still didn't see her. Finally, she stood.

"You done already?" James asked, standing with her.

"No, I'm just—" she was sure now that Ava wasn't at the bird table. She pretended the flutter in her belly had nothing to do with it.

"She's not there," James reiterated.

"What?" Tarun stood, too.

"Ava," Winta clarified. "She isn't with them. Good. It's about time."

"Oh, wipe that silly grin off your face," JiSoo groused, stabbing her pork. "Maybe they sent her on an errand or something. Doesn't mean she finally came to her senses."

"Or maybe she did," Tarun suggested.

"Why don't we go up right now and see? We don't have to sit here and debate." JiSoo dropped her fork again and daintily wiped her lips, her eyes challenging Winta to go with her.

"Fine!" Winta didn't have to be asked twice and hurried out with JiSoo.

They hurried toward Indigo. One hoping to be right, the other dearly wishing she was wrong.

In her room, Ava stood by the side while two female attendants ransacked everything she owned. They emptied her closet on the bed, shoes overturned, her mattress pulled up and inspected. Geez. This would take her forever to reorganize. How rude.

"Where are your bags?" the grim-faced attendant asked.

Ava solemnly pointed at the top of her closet, silently cursing whoever stole the crown for interrupting her life like this. She didn't need more chores, and now she'd have to arrange the entire room again...including JiSoo's section as a peace offering.

The taller attendant pulled down Ava's suitcase —the large brown one—and placed it on the bed.

The next events played out in slow motion— Ava's brain unable to process what she witnessed.

"Got it!" the attendant yelled, smiling. "Tell the others."

"What?" Ava took a step back. "That's not possible.... I didn't put that there!" she denied, but it fell on deaf ears.

"Come with me, Miss."

"No, no, you don't understand. I just came back to this room an hour ago. I didn't put that there!" she couldn't bring herself to say "steal."

"I know, deny it all you want. Fact is, we found it in your room, in your bag, so you have to come with me. The headmistress is waiting."

Ava didn't even pay attention to which one was speaking to her. "Please, you have to believe me, this is my first time even seeing it up close."

The taller attendant's face remained stony as she advanced on Ava. "Miss, don't make me force you."

Just then, JiSoo and Winta barged into the room, temporarily distracting the attendant.

"What's going on here!" neat-freak JiSoo demanded at the disaster that was her room.

"JiSoo, Winta...tell her I didn't do it, please!" Ava was frantic at this point.

"She didn't do it," they said together without question. What good friends.

"Miss?" the attendant prompted, not interested in hearing Ava's friends defend her.

"You heard her! She's my roommate!" Ava pointed to JiSoo. "She was here. Ask her! I haven't touched that bag since I got here." Ava's voice spiked feverishly.

The attendant had had enough. She pushed Ava toward the door.

"Where are you taking her?" Winta demanded.

They trailed behind Ava and the attendant, begging her to listen. By then, most of the trainees were returning to their dorms from dinner, and they gathered to watch Ava getting dragged away.

Ahead, Ava saw Elaine and her flock grinning widely. Elaine winked deviously at Ava when she got close.

Ava's stomach dropped, and she felt like she might vomit. Too late, she realized she'd fallen into Elaine's trap.

28

Ava was still in shock even after they escorted her to the isolation room—yes, the school had an isolation room—and left her there alone.

This couldn't be happening, not to her. Ava shivered in the corner, avoiding the bed and even the food they had served her. It wasn't necessarily cold in the room, but her nerves were a mess.

She'd tried so hard to fit in. She'd even lost her best friends, the only people in the whole school who'd actually been nice to her for no reason other than they wanted to.

They'd tried to warn her. And after all of their warnings, which she refused to listen to, they still came rushing back to her. And what did Tarun think about her now?

Her dream had been thrown in the toilet and flushed. She would never graduate from Animage Academy now. What would her mother say? What would she even do with her life after this? And this is all assuming she wasn't on her way to jail. Surely, they would be kind to a sixteen-year-old, right?

She sniffled, tasting salt. She wiped her cheeks furiously, only for fresh tears to run down.

If only...

Oh, whatever.

There was no time for 'if only's. None of that would help her now, anyway.

But her mind refused to listen. If only she'd seen the signs. If only she paid attention to how the flock treated her when Elaine wasn't around. If only she'd been more observant about Elaine's mannerisms.

Elaine, she laughed bitterly, was an evil genius. There was no doubt in her mind exactly who'd stabbed her in the back. Ava certainly couldn't confirm, but she knew it in her gut. She couldn't even allow herself to feel betrayed, because she was the one stupid enough to fall into the trap.

As she thought of Elaine, she proceeded to get more furious. Now, she would have to leave. Elaine had won, and would probably find a way to seduce Tarun.

"NO!" she screamed, feeling a little unhinged.

Winta and JiSoo had tried to talk sense into her, but she wouldn't listen. Now she'd ruined everything. "NOOO!" she screamed again as she started to rock back and forth. Yes, she realized she was losing it. But she didn't care. Now she'd never learn about her father, and she'd probably never even have real friends like that again. She could feel the tingling in her belly start to take over.

Crap, her emotions were getting the better of her. Maybe she was about to have a panic attack. Or maybe lose herself in a fit of rage. Whatever. She didn't care.

She decided to give in and let it roll. It didn't matter if she shifted in that stupid little room, anyway.

"Why!?" She stood up and screamed out of pure frustration, pulling at her hair. "WHY!?"

The backs of her hands grew warm and she could feel her muscles stretching along with her bones.

The door to her isolation room opened, and one of the school attendants she'd never seen before poked his head in, probably to see what the commotion was all about. She was running around screaming and yelling after all.

Ava's fury thrummed through her, feeling something else deep within her. Her bones creaked, shattered, and rearranged. That's when she fell on all fours, morphing into her cat. But it didn't stop there this time. Her hands and feet stretched and elongated. Ava's head exploded in an extreme pressure that was almost pleasurable. A tingling sensation swept across her forehead.

In the back of her mind, she heard the attendant scream out, but she couldn't tell what he said. That's when a bright purplish light, powerful and blinding, filled the room.

In that burst of pure light, her transformation was immediate and absolute.

Regaining her bearings, she moved to a standing position and looked around. She wasn't in her tabby cat form. Definitely not. Her head bumped the ceiling. But she could *feel* what she was. She didn't have to look down at her hooves to know. She let out a loud whinny.

She was a unicorn.

29

Without thinking twice, Ava trotted right out the door, having to bend way down to squeeze through the door frame. The attendant had run off, so she decided to see herself out.

She wanted to be outside. It called to her. Coming to a staircase, she realized she was in a dank basement. That just wouldn't do for a unicorn. Leaping to the top of the stairs, she thrust her horn through the door and broke herself out into the open.

Relieved to be free.

After a frightened employee came rushing to share the news, Headmistress Levine rushed to the basement to see what all the commotion was about. When she found the basement door completely shattered, she followed the neighing sound to the courtyard, heart racing.

"Ava Carrington," she whispered, staring at the magnificent creature before her. The animal's horn glinted beautifully in the sunlight.

"I told you I didn't do it!" Ava screamed at the headmistress, sending a burst of purple light out all around her.

Levine blinked, impressed that Ava was already able to speak in that form. The old griffin woman traipsed over to her, raised her hands, palms outward, and patted Ava's front thigh.

"Do you hear me?" Ava demanded. "I didn't steal the crown!"

"I know—"

"Why don't you believe me!?"

"I just said I know you didn't steal it, Carrington. I believe you." The headmistress cut short the unicorn's tirade.

Ava stiffened and looked back at Levine. "You believe me now?"

"You are a pure creature. You cannot lie." Levine stared back at her, point blank.

Ava shook her head back and forth. "What? I've lied plenty of times in my life."

"Your full unicorn power didn't manifest until recently. That's why you can suddenly heal," Levine explained. "Remember when I let you go after Elaine caught you in the library? I told you to meet me in five days. I realized what you were up to, and I had talked to some of the professors. I wanted to take a few days to prepare the information. I was planning to talk to you about this when we met up."

"So you knew this would happen?"

"I knew this transformation would take place eventually, but I didn't necessarily think it would be today!" Levine exclaimed, a little laugh at the end of her sentence.

"I've had enough of Elaine." Ava stamped her hoof. "She planted that crown in my room."

"And she will be dealt with."

"So I'm really not in trouble?"

"No," Levine answered simply. The girl was stunningly beautiful in this form. All white with a purple mane sprinkled with silver and gold. A shimmering ivory white horn. But still-very-catlike eyes—a very unusual feline look on an equine.

"So this is why I was accepted to this school? It was never about being a tabby cat, was it?" Ava asked.

"Correct." Levine kept her expression solemn. "You are what's called a dual shifter, or in some texts, a dyad. But it would take special training for your gift to come forth."

"You let me suffer through almost an entire semester, endure all the bullies, and for what? You could've told me about this at the beginning!" She stamped both her front hooves this time.

"No, Ava, it was better you discovered this for yourself. If you'd known in advance, you would have tried to force the gift, and it would have taken you much longer to grow comfortable. Only when you reach into your truest self will the second form emerge. I had nothing to do with this."

Ava pranced back and forth a few times. Levine was truly grateful she had exited through the back entrance of the school where no one was around to see her.

"Wait, what about all the others? Everyone here who shifts into a lame animal? Why are they here? Like James, or JiSoo, or those guinea-pig twins..."

Levine chose her words carefully. Unicorns had a knack for detecting lies. "They were admitted so we could compete with the new school."

"What? What new school?"

"There is a new shifter school above. In New

Zealand, actually. It's a lot to explain, but we had to step up our game."

"Right." Ava didn't say anything else.

The headmistress knew she had more explaining to do, but for now, she just wanted to stand back and appreciate the beauty that was Ava Carrington in her unicorn form.

30

The semester was close to an end.

Ava and her friends anxiously waited for the announcement for the finals. They would all start training for them at the beginning of the second semester. It was all anyone could talk about. No one knew what form it would take, so they all practiced harder, read textbooks, memorized notes.

When the announcement finally came, Ava was excited to learn that they would take place this year in the form of a talent show. Boy, did she have a lot of talent to show now!

Yesterday, a letter had come for her, confirming what she already knew. Her mother warned severely to stop searching for her father. Ava wasn't sure she'd obey.

JiSoo and Winta weren't particularly welcoming that next morning when she slunk back to beg for forgiveness, but still they all sat together now.

"JiSoo, what should her punishment be?" Winta had asked petulantly.

"She should carry our backpacks for the rest of the semester."

Ava groaned. When they glared at her, she changed it to a charming smile with a little wink.

"What else?" Winta smirked. "There has to be more she can do."

"You're enjoying this, aren't you?" Ava grumbled.

"Hush, it's not time for you to speak yet," JiSoo pressed her finger to her lips. "Got it! Our laundries. She has to do those, too."

Ava laughed. "It's laundry, not laundries."

"You aren't supposed to be talking, remember?" JiSoo stuck out her tongue.

"Oh, shut up, both of you," Winta said, raising her arms outward.

Ava rushed into them without hesitation.

"Wait, wait, I gotta get in on this, too..." JiSoo yelped as she wrapped her arms (as far as they could go) around both Winta and Ava.

When the girls finally released each other, JiSoo looked a little tearful. "Allergies... Did you change your shampoo?" JiSoo grumbled, rubbing her eyes.

"Careful!" Winta and Ava yelled, but it was too late. JiSoo had already lost both eyes again....

The second semester came and went.

The school competition had taken place, but it was just the Animage students competing against one another, and it didn't involve first-years, so it didn't hold Ava's attention the way it did many others' in the school.

She had attended with her friends, along with Tarun and James, but she didn't really get the rules. All she knew was a pack of senior wolves had come in first. Tarun and James had been ecstatic about that, as they were rooting for the winning team, but Ava didn't really understand why. Whatever. Boys and their sports.

Her relationship, or whatever it was, with Tarun had certainly grown. He was proud to be seen with her, but they never fully recovered from the tensions of her leaving the group for Elaine. They were still friends, and Ava desperately wanted more, and she suspected Tarun did as well, but they hadn't so much as kissed again. But that was okay; he was still by her side most of the time, and Ava could be patient. Especially for someone as wonderful as Tarun.

Now, after months of prepping and dozens of grueling one-on-one sessions with both Professor Bills and Sir Waters, and even a few with Head-mistress Levine herself, Ava was ready for the finals.

Backstage, Ava peeked through the curtain. This would be the first time she saw a crowd of this size, aside from when the students gathered together in the auditorium. But this was different —this time *she* was going to be the one on stage in front of the school auditorium.

Ava still hadn't told any of her friends, even Winta, about her second form. Headmistress Levine had insisted she keep it a secret even from them. It was painful, and she daily felt like she was lying to them, but then she reminded herself that she was a pure creature who *couldn't* lie. Had her friends asked her directly, "Are you a dual shifter who can transform into both a tabby cat and a unicorn?", she certainly would have said yes.

But that didn't happen. Because that would be ridiculous.

The wolf on stage was currently standing on his hind legs. Ava saw Professor Bills grind his teeth. She swallowed, feeling bad for the shifter. Winta and JiSoo stood on either side of her.

"Whoa, that's bad," JiSoo said through clenched teeth.

Ava couldn't disagree with her.

They had one task, and that was to convince the audience they could survive and thrive in both animal and human form. But mostly animal. Add into that the fact they needed to show off their talents and skills as much as possible for higher marks. A wolf standing on his hind legs wasn't much to clap for.

Just as she thought: the applause was minimal at best. The shifter transformed back to human and left the stage, but Ava imagined if he'd still been in his wolf form, his tail would be between his legs.

The next shifter in line, Ava was pleased to see, was Priya, the little girl she'd met before school had even started.

Excited, and interested to see her again, Ava squinted to get a better look. Priya was impressive. Ava knew she shifted into a little canary bird, but clearly Priya hadn't been lying when she mentioned her father showing her lots of tricks already. Because she could shift only her arms into giant yellow wings and fly around the auditorium. After a few more minutes of theatrical tricks such as flips and dive bombs, Priya landed to receive her rousing applause. Even Ava clapped for her little friend.

Winta and JiSoo weren't speaking now. She knew they were nervous. Winta was concerned she was going to trash the stage and hurt someone, and JiSoo just desperately hoped her eyes wouldn't pop out and roll off the edge to be trampled.

"Ava..." someone called from behind her.

She swiveled to see who it was. "Tarun... Hi..."

As he approached, as always, her insides turned to mush.

"You got this," he encouraged her, sliding his hand around her waist and pulling her into a—somewhat intimate—hug.

"Easy for you to say. You aced it with flying colors."

"And so will you."

"Seriously though," Ava went on. "The crowd stood and clapped like crazy. I haven't seen them get that excited for anyone else."

"I know, I'm amazing."

"And humble, of course."

"I'm Tarun, could I BE any more awesome?"

Ava laughed from deep within her heart at his Chandler impression.

He grinned in his usual disarming way.

"I still think you're more like Ross though," she said, trying to look as serious as possible.

"And would that make you Rachel?"

"Yuck! No! I like Monica." She pushed her hand into his chest playfully.

"Then I'm definitely Chandler." He put his hand over hers on his chest.

Her breath caught in her throat. "What are you trying to say?" she asked him quietly so the others couldn't hear her.

Without warning, Tarun slipped his other hand behind Ava's neck and brought her face toward his as he lowered down and kissed her.

Suddenly, Ava couldn't feel her legs. She knew they were rooted to the spot, but the only thing she was aware of were her lips against his. She returned this kiss even more eagerly than she had the last one, and it had been entirely too long. A whole semester, in fact. But definitely worth the wait. He was even more delicious than she remembered.

Allowing him to explore her mouth as she explored his, she reached both arms around his neck and pressed herself into him as tightly as possible, wishing she would never have to let him go.

"Guys, it's my turn now!" JiSoo announced.

Ava and Tarun snapped apart, very confused at first, until they realized JiSoo meant it was her turn on stage, not for a kiss!

"Oh!" they both exclaimed together.

Then, with an impressive amount of confidence, JiSoo went bounding out onto the stage while her friends watched.

Tarun reached down and clasped Ava's hand in his, giving it a little squeeze. Ava squeezed him back.

JiSoo turned and faced the crowd and, like she had so many times before, transformed into a pug. She pranced around on the stage, caught food thrown in the air, rolled around, and let out a series of barks to the tune of Twinkle Twinkle Little Star. All without losing a single eyeball.

Ava wondered how she would be scored because it offered little in the way of combat skills, but she was a pug after all. No matter how much she trained, pugs just weren't built for combat. And no one could hold that against her.

And she was well received indeed. Even grouchy Professor Bills couldn't resist smiling at cute little JiSoo.

"Next!"

Three shifters later, and it was Winta's turn.

She moved to the stage, too, trembling. Then, turning away from the crowd, she opened her mouth, still in her human form, and trumpeted...*loudly*. The crowd went wild.

During the raucous screaming, she transformed into her elephant, marched forward amid the screams, trumpeted again, and, flapping her ears, she went back across the stage where a wooden ball waited for her.

Like an elephant in a three-ring circus, she stepped onto the ball, balanced herself carefully, and, finally, trumpeted again.

"Go, Winta!" Ava called out to encourage her best friend, but it didn't seem like she needed it. She had done a phenomenal job.

After transforming back, she took her bow and returned to her friends, beaming.

Ava was the last shifter in her class to get on stage. Levine had planned it that way.

"You got this, Babe." Tarun gave her a kiss on the cheek.

She didn't smile or say anything. She just took a deep breath and waltzed out there.

So many faces. She stood there getting her bearings for a moment before morphing into her tabby. She twirled in the air, slashed through it with her claws.

She had practiced that over and over, yet the crowd remained silent. Bills sat unimpressed. Sir Waters yawned.

Ava took a deep breath. She still had several

more cat tricks planned, but decided to change her routine in a heartbeat.

Letting the light take over, she reached for her soul, her true form, and shifted....

After the long, charged silence was broken by Bills letting out an eardrum-splitting whistle, all Ava had to do was stand there, horn glistening and tail swishing, before she received her standing ovation.

"Oh, great. It's you with all the bags," Paul groused as he looked Ava up and down.

She had just stepped off the Animage ship at the port where she, Michaela, and the others from the Miami branch were to meet Paul to escort them home.

Saying goodbye to her friends had been heart wrenching, but they were all encouraged by the knowledge they would see each other again in a few months. They had all passed the finals with flying colors and were to be welcomed back for their second year at Animage Academy.

And although her friends were upset with her for not disclosing her second transformation for an entire semester, they understood Levine had sworn her to secrecy. She smiled to herself. It was probably easy to forgive a unicorn.

It had only been two days since she'd revealed herself on that stage, and she noticed a major difference in the way all her classmates treated her immediately. She didn't know what this would mean for her and her training in the upcoming years, but she was excited to find out. Ava was no longer the meek little kitty. She was Ava Carrington: dyad and unicorn shifter!

"I see you dyed your hair," Paul observed. "You been hanging out with Michaela?" He nodded his head toward the snarky, pink-haired wolf shifter.

Ava shook her head. "No, my hair turned this color on its own after my second transformation took over." She touched the ends of her hair, which were no longer that dingy brown she hated. Instead, her hair was a deep purple hue. It had turned that color slowly over the course of the past several months. She didn't even realize it was happening at first, but then JiSoo pointed it out to her, wondering what in the world was going on. Even Ava was confused until Levine explained it to her.

Paul's eyes grew as wide as saucers. "Purple hair! Second transformation!? It's *you* then!"

Ava tilted her head and asked, "What do you

mean?" Even though she already had a pretty good idea what he was referring to.

"I heard we had one at the school," he said with awe in his voice. "I can't believe it's you. You know what they're saying, right?"

"What's that?" Ava raised a curious eyebrow.

Paul grabbed her brown bag from her and leaned in close, as if he didn't want anyone else to hear him. "That you're the last unicorn shifter on Earth."

Ava puckered her lips at that very sad fact. Her first year at Animage had turned out to be quite the year indeed. And, boy, did she have a lot to tell her mom when she got home.

END OF YEAR ONE

ALSO BY QATARINA & ORA WANDERS

Find out what Ava will do with her unicorn powers...

Order Animage Academy Year 2 NOW!

ABOUT THE AUTHORS

Qatarina & Ora Wanders are a fantasy-book-loving mother-daughter duo.

Ora published her first book, *Children of the Elements: A Steampunk Adventure*, at 10 years old, and has no intention of stopping there!

Qatarina already has a number of books in her arsenal—both fiction and non-fiction.

When these two aren't *wandering* around the world together (pun intended!) in search of exotic experiences, they are probably sitting at home having adventures by reading books next to each other on the couch...or maybe playing with their two guinea pigs: Mochi and Edgar Allan Pig

If you are interested in hanging out with them on social media, you can join their Facebook reader group at: Qat's Wandering Word Nerds and find them at...

- facebook.com/qatwrites
- twitter.com/qatwanders
- instagram.com/qat_wanders
- amazon.com/author/orawanders
- bookbub.com/authors/qatarinawanders
- pinterest.com/Qatwanders

OTHER BOOKS BY ORA WANDERS
Children of the Elements Book One

Rise from Slumber: The Exousia Chronicles
Book One

PLEASE HELP!

If you enjoyed this book, please, help us out by leaving us a helpful review on Amazon (as well as Goodreads and BookBub if you are on those platforms).

We publish these books independently, so reviews are really the only way our books will be found by other potential readers.

Thanks so much!

~Qat and Ora

ACKNOWLEDGMENTS

Special thanks to TJ Marquis, Dandy Anwuacha, and Dorcia Beland for your storyline and editing brilliance, and Loraine Van Tonder for this GAWDJUSS cover! <3

Made in the USA
Coppell, TX
03 May 2021